I0760292

Tranquility and Other Myths

Tranquility and Other Myths

By

The Hourlings

Editor Donna Royston

Art, Cover, and Design John Dwight

Publishing Martin Wilsey

Published in the U.S.A.
by Tannhauser Press
www.tannhauserpress.com

ISBN 978-1-945994-32-6
Third Edition, December 2018

Contents

INTRODUCTION

CHRONICLES FROM EARTH

MARY ELLEN GAVIN

Mary Ellen Gavin is a literary agent, editor, and writing teacher. She specializes in historical fiction and her work is available on Amazon.com, including ***Secrets of the Apple Tree Tavern*** and ***Hiding Places at Barrington Hall: Hannelley & Hennessey Investigations.*** She is currently working on a science fiction novel called ***All Is Well In Nirvana.***

In ***Principia Mathematica***, Sir Isaac Newton's opus on natural knowledge, he says in part "*In philosophical discussions, we ought to step back from our senses, and consider* *things themselves, distinct from what are only perceptible measures of them.*" Mary Ellen's tale of distant visitors explores the distinction between perceptions and reality. And it serves as an introduction to the group of writers and friends whose work fills these pages.

The final report from Commander Lucien075

The three of us entered this universe two days ago, blue-planet time, and parked the Mother Ship XKE behind the dirt-ball satellite they refer to as their Moon. It offered cover from the planet we now know as Earth.

We dropped a Bubble Craft out of the XKE and easily passed invisibly through all the planet's security rays to reach the Dulles Airport. It offered an empty runway during their dark hours and we were able to park our vehicle without detection. Once away from the landing strip, we shape-shifted from translucent to short Greys. That was when we were the most vulnerable. We needed to locate our package sent ahead with clothes, money and identification. Earth is on high alert for Greys. It seems our predecessors may have overstepped what was asked of them during previous missions.

We got a blip and found that it was originating in the main building that was already locked. Standing only three feet with only two black eyes, we had to stay well hidden while canvassing the area. Finally, 076 and 077 found an unlocked back door and we dashed inside, grateful that our eyes do see in the dark. The blip led us to a door marked as the lost & found room. It was filled with all sorts of containers and we wondered, *How many other planets had sent emissaries here?*

We reviewed our mission: scout the capital and invade the brain trust that keeps this planet from spinning into extinction.

After a day of research, we learned their habits. Reading their news from the *Washington Post*, we found there are two types of humans: male and female. Both share the same lifestyle but have different mindsets and utilize opposite strategies.

The males stand taller and are physically more robust. Acting openly, they easily express themselves without rancor and wear belts. The females are physically shorter, curvier and have a bust line that holds up their clothing. Acting covertly, they spin the truth and use undercover moves to manipulate through cunning and cuteness.

Naturally, we chose to copy the gender most like our own species when assembling our new earth bodies. Looking in the mirror, we rushed out to go clothes shopping and found bargains galore on purses, makeup, perfume and shoes.

Searching their electronic intelligence, we realized that the scribes here wield power by putting thoughts into people's minds. In that way, humans act according to the plans of the writers. Finding where those genius minds hang out via Meetup.com was a stroke of luck. *The Hourlings* came up immediately and we were able to join online without a blood test.

There was a lot of recon needed before attending their next meeting. We scanned the new writing pieces that four of the membership provided for review and dissected each work for hidden agenda. To be clear, there is a lot that they write about that we three do not understand. For example, we had to look up the words… fiction and fantasy. Reading their code book, called a dictionary, we found their definitions for the two words, but still we wondered what they meant.

How could something be imaginative but not true, or not true but might be true in the future?

That is when we were able to grasp the true nature of their brilliance. Writers know their way around words. No doubt, they hide their secret communication under the banner of fiction and fantasy to avoid detection. How imaginative! The mind saboteurs here work out in the open, sending thoughts and ideas to their readers.

Searching further on Meetup.com we found that those very smart writers would allow other very smart writers to physically appear at their meetings. They openly ask new members to join them and share ideas. And that is when we decided to present ourselves in the embodiment of famous authors already revered on this planet.

Again searching their electronic intelligence, we found listings of successful writers. Lucien076 adopted the personae of Ellen DeGeneres because 076 likes her no-fuss haircut. 077

took on a younger version of one Mary Higgins Clark, as her books were easy to read and commit to memory in case we were interrogated.

I found a lesser known writer on what they call The Web, who goes by the name of Mary Ellen Gavin. Since we would be walking into their meeting place together, one of us had to be a new face in the company of the two very successful authors.

))) ● ● ● ● ● ● (((

Ellen and Mary were up all night conversing in their new voices that were polar opposite: Ellen stayed bouncy and fun while Mary kept an air of sophistication.

At 4:00 am Earth Time, they began to try on clothes and makeup until this planet spun back into the warm rays of their star.

Being the not-so-successful Mary Ellen, I was able to rest and spend the time quietly preparing for the writing group. Our infiltration mission was to seek out their goals for power and learn how they planned implementation. Therefore, it would be easier for me to host the questioning. And that's when a stark realization came to me: fame has its drawbacks.

One minute to ten, we walked into the bakery in Sterling, Virginia. The discreet instructions were to look for a dragon flag waving atop the tables gathered together to seat twelve. And there they were, nine humans sitting around that banner of a dragon who had fire shooting out of its mouth. Just the sight of it made me wonder if there might not be a dark dungeon where they kept the real dragon.

Spotting our entrance, all nine stopped talking and eating. Curious faces turned in unison to watch our approach. This would be our first contact. As I led the way, I felt ready to front for my two colleagues who I sensed were already losing their nerve.

"Hello!" A pretty dark-haired female said. "Welcome. We were waiting for you. Now we'll go around the table, introduce ourselves, and talk about our stories."

As we sat down, the door flew open behind us and a smiling young lady drove a personal vehicle. Surprised to see a motorized throne, especially one where a fuzzy bear rode backwards, the three of us could only assume she was royalty.

Pulling up to the tables, we could see her beautiful skin and sparkling eyes. When she looked at each one of us with a coy smile we could not help, but smile back. Or, perhaps it was the jaunty hat atop her silky hair.

Seeing the others light up and hearing her introduction, we knew Shea to be a princess. Telepathically we agreed that her beauty could be traced back to the planet Demure, once a paradise until pirates began kidnapping the loveliest of the maidens. There must be a legend in Shea's ancestry. I will look for it in her short story: ***MONEY TREE***.

Next to the lovely Shea was the happy face of Bill, whose big eyes opened wide when he laughed. His genuine appreciation of people made me think his human lineage might have been crossed with canine. Bill was that sincere. He admitted to being a copywriter. I could never see Bill copying anyone's writing. Can't wait to read his story: ***MAGIC ACT***.

Next to Bill was the handsome Jeremy, whose beaming dark eyes and shaved head were reminiscent of the magnificent Egyptian rulers. Jeremy was secretive, waltzing around his personal data. He did mention a military attachment and how he would disappear on some weekends. I sent a tele-alert to Ellen and Mary: Jeremy is probably a trained assassin, but he can be trusted. Looking forward to reading his story: ***HEIR RING***.

Next to the mysterious Jeremy was the very attractive Donna, whose thick mane of white hair was a beauty reserved for animals in the wild. Donna's ancient ancestry may have crossed paths with the wolf. Adding to her appeal was her smart thinking and ability to share in story form. Her knowledge of authors makes me anxious to read: ***THE FIRST CENSOR'S STATEMENT***.

Next to Donna was Liz, the likeable female who had welcomed us. Her soft eyes were so transparent that she could never lie or be deceptive. Liz showed lots of attention to the membership that now included us. Excited about the upcoming anthology, Liz invited us to pen a short story and said we could read her story: ***EMISSARY - TUITION MONEY***.

Next to the lovely Liz was John, intelligently handsome, whose insouciant smile and intense eyes hinted at extrasensory powers not likely to be found on this planet. When a couple of static bursts crossed my brain, I felt someone was beaming. Scanning each face to find the broadcaster, my eyes kept stopping at John. Funny how he seemed to know I was headed his way. John worried me and I could not wait to read his story: ***THE DARKEST EVENING.***

Next to John was Marty, who kept his head down in a secretive manner while introducing himself as a first-time author of the novel *Still Falling*. Finally, he looked up and I saw a no-nonsense guy with a disarming smile. As he told us about his story, I listened closely. Marty knew how to spin a story and I wanted to read more: ***DOCTOR CLARK LOVED PIZZA***.

Next to Marty was Chris, a handsome young man with a warm smile. His features were so photogenic that he reminded me of the young actors who advertise their acting ability in the Hollywood magazine, *Variety*. Staring at Chris, I began to suspect that he might not be a writer and wondered if he might be an actor disguised as a writer. Reading the tabloids, I had learned how actors secretly join literary groups to seek out the best writers. Then they turn those talented scribes into slave writers, churning out story pages written only for that actor. I believed a certain Tom Cruise was rumored to be one of those *Vampire Actors*… and I noticed now how Chris and Tom shared a resemblance. I will study his story: ***TUTTLEBEE, THE SCRIVENER***.

Next to Chris was Susan, a beautiful blond female with an easy smile. Anyone could see that she was forthright and full of fun. We laughed along with her as she shared some of her life experiences. Then she got serious. It was time to talk about her entry into the anthology and we listened.

Ellen and Mary must have picked Susan's brain because they were already tele-screaming in my head. They asked why the word, Giants, was in her title. Did Susan not know the Giants had already conquered most of the planets in the seventh universe?

I tele-shouted back that Susan did not look like a Giant, and it was doubtful that she had ties to them. Still, I was forced to put Susan on a Watch List. I calmed down and told Ellen and Mary that we'd know more when we read Susan's short story entry: ***IMAGINE GIANTS***.

Next to Susan was Nathan, a lean young man who was very tall. He stayed quiet, but let his eyes roam around the table. Coming across as a nice man, he was hard to judge and I realized why. Nathan seemed to be the epitome of a writer. A writer who went to school to actually study writing. Not just a wannabe, but one who actually put in the time to learn from the greats. We will know more when we read Nathan's entry: ***A WORLD WITHOUT TAXI DRIVERS***.

Next to Nathan was Rachael, who was young and smart and pretty. Her carefree manner was endearing, but she stayed alert. Her eyes kept sizing up each one of us. Still, I did not hear any alerts in my head. Ellen and Mary stayed calm as Rachael introduced herself and talked about off-planet mining. That was when I took a second look at Rachael, wondering which planet she was referring to. I am anxious to read: ***CHEERS***.

Next to Rachael was Stephanie. She had perfect features and was always doing comparatives. Sophisticated and intelligent, Stephanie used precise language with correct answers. What female does that? Stephanie will be joining Susan and Alec on the Watch List. ***SOLSTICE MAGIC***.

Next to Stephanie was Katherine, refined and classy with natural blond hair. Her daring never reached overconfidence. She came across as a true writer who was always questioning her work. What? No writer does that! Katherine is going on the Watch List. ***LOVESICK***.

Next to Katherine and sitting to my right was David, whose curious blue eyes kept sneaking peeks at the three of us by dropping his eyelids so we did not notice. David no doubt thought I was not paying attention, but he was wrong. My alarms went off every time his eyes wandered our way. For some reason, his stealth was disturbing my estrogen levels… a newly acquired sensing system that came with my female kit.

He was discussing the moon and must have seen my fear of exposure of the XKE hiding up there. He asked me if I understood the orbital relationship between the Moon and Earth. All three of us nodded, but David did not believe us. He changed the subject to his short story written for the anthology and I am looking forward to it: ***WINTER ROSES***.

It was my turn and I introduced myself. "I'm Mary Ellen and I write stories that are not true, but entertain me as I write them. I guess you could call me a liar who needs entertainment." Everyone laughed, to my surprise. I followed with, "We came here to learn the secrets of your writing." They thought that was even funnier.

It was Mary's turn and she said, "You might know me, or maybe you've read some of my books?"

Blank faces stared back at her, perhaps not recognizing her younger version.

Mary was frozen by her pride. Didn't I tell her not to stray from the formula?

Ellen, sitting next to Mary, picked up the conversation. "Surely you recognize me. I have put out a couple of books telling about my life that you might have read."

Silence.

"Here's a clue. I like to open my daytime show dancing up and down the aisles."

It was so quiet, we could hear the conversations at the tables around us. Ellen looked shocked, seeing no recognition.

Shoulders shrugged and heads kept shaking around the table. A few murmured how they did not really watch daytime TV. The rest picked up their cellular phones and either scanned for data or sent messages. Their fast fingers, tapping upon the screens was amazing. All communication at the table ceased, as if this stoppage to connect with their electronic world was a ritual everyone knew about except us.

This was becoming embarrassing. Either the members were having fun with the images of Mary and Ellen or they truly did not recognize two of their own. Again, I congratulated myself on choosing the lowly Mary Ellen Gavin. My pride was intact.

Liz looked up and said, "It is interesting that you three share the same two names."

All heads nodded, waiting for an explanation. I saw the frozen faces of my comrades. They had nothing to say so I jump in with a feeble tale. "True. It's kinda how we became friends at a writers' conference. They kept mixing us up because our first names."

The members bought it and their pleasant laughter relieved our tension.

Table conversation stopped, as most were finishing their breakfasts and clearing their debris. We three could only watch as the others shared small tidbits of news from their daily lives. I felt a sense of loss for not having a daily life. It is not something offered in the universe where we originate.

I stood up and excused myself. Mary and Ellen did the same and followed me to the lady's room. It was empty. Ellen barred the door while Mary and I grabbed the stalls.

"What's going on?" Ellen sounded upset. "I thought everyone loved me!"

"What did you expect?" I asked her, in a voice of reason.

"I thought they'd want to know personal stuff about us or ask us to perform."

Mary spoke up. "Writers are odd creatures who create in the dark."

I tried to tell them the truth. "Forget your pride. We're here to learn about them, not for them to learn about us. Next meeting? We'll come as fresh faces."

Returning, I saw there were more tables added and new people had arrived. We took our seats and smiled, but I got the strange sensation that we were under observation.

Liz reminded us how the group meets every week to share readings and sets an ancient timer in the middle of the tables. All eyes watched the blue crystals sliding through the glass stem to count time. My colleagues tele-messaged me that this might be yet another sign that we are right about these writers. They may not be from this planet, either. The proof was in front of us. Everyone in this universe and the next knew that dragons only survived on the Dragonian Planets and live there still.

These writers knew secrets from the past and no doubt from the future. Did they plan to implement old and futuristic magic into this planet's modern day? Or, were they here as scouts for an overthrow and perhaps bringing a few of the dragons with them?

I made a mental note to study all civilizations that ever used crystal timekeeping. Perhaps, we might spot where the mystical writers came from.

Liz invited Dyson's story to be the first for a *critique*. That word itself sounds garish behind the scraping of cutlery. In fact, the three of us had brought sharp letter openers hidden in our new purses just in case a fight broke out.

A frenzied discussion began. Vigorous, even chaotic at times, but amicable all the same. There were questions about characters and plot, Dyson's purpose behind certain things, and where he intended the piece to go. Folks told him what worked well, and what was distracting. They even had ideas for things to put in. And Dyson absorbed the feedback, scribbling intricate details into a book for notes. His pen flicked the air, licked the pages as it went. He seemed at times to parry, dodge, and riposte as he wrote.

The females sat quiet. We were felines watching a dog fight. I believed we shared the same strategy: let them battle it out. We would take on the winner.

Several more writers showed up and gave the three of us the once-over. All the while, more and more were communicating via their electronic instruments. I started to believe they were talking to each other.

The next three story reviews went the same way. When the clock struck twelve noon, Earth Time, we all left with warm goodbyes till next week. The three of us are fascinated by what takes place at The Bakery every week. Which is why we are not leaving. We feel it is our duty to stay and report from the enemy's camp.

Signing out, Lucien075 now known as Mary Ellen Gavin.

The Book of the Full Moon

The moon is a friend for the lonesome to talk to.

- Carl Sandburg

Watching the moon at midnight, solitary in the high sky, I knew myself completely, no part left out.

- Izumi Shikibu

DOCTOR CLARK LOVED PIZZA

MARTIN WILSEY

Martin Wilsey is the author of the ***Solstice 31 Saga***, including the novel ***Still Falling***, where a member of an interplanetary crew is marooned on a strange moon. In addition to being a storyteller, Martin is a hunter, photographer, rabble rouser, and frightener of children. To keep himself off the streets, Martin works as a research scientist for a government funded think tank, studying exotic new technologies.

In this selection, Martin offers the story of a pizza delivery guy and his best customer, one Doctor Clark. Franz Kafka said,

DOCTOR CLARK LOVED PIZZA

"So long as you have food in your mouth, you have solved all questions for the time being." I suspect, however, that ole Doctor Clark was pondering a few things even as he ate.

Look. Mike, don't screw this up." Mr. Delio said to Mike as he expertly tossed the pizza dough into the air, shaping a perfect large crust.

It wasn't the kind of thing he expected to hear on the first day of his first job. He had made eleven pizza deliveries already that day. He had over $70 in tips and it was only just 5pm.

"Dr. Clark is my best customer. Two large pies a week for the last eight years." He slid the perfectly formed crust down to Peg at the sauce station and started another. "He's an odd one but follow the instructions on that damn card and you will get a $20 tip."

Mike looked at the laminated 3 by 5 card in his hand. He smiled as he tried not to mention the misspellings.

- Knock and go in annocing LOUD 'Delio's Pizza'.
- Go in and put the pizza on the kitchen island.
- Put the six pack of Mt. Dew in fridge.
- Take the $20 yo find in the fridge.
- Say out loud "Thank you Dr. Clark"

- DO NOT correct him if he calls you Dave.
- If the trash barel is full drag to curb.

"Mr. Delio, who is Dave?" Mike asked shyly.

"That's my son David. He was the first delivery guy for Dr. Clark back when this started." Mr. Delio slipped the next formed pie to Peg, another employee at Delio's, and then stepped aside with Mike out of earshot of Peg and his other employees. "Mike, I picked you for this because I have known your parents your whole life. I have watched you grow up and I know you are a good kid."

Mike was wondering at the conspiratorial tone.

"Don't be weirded out by the old guy. And try to watch out for him. You and Tom Wilkins are the only people he sees these days. Do you know Tom?" Mr. Delio asked as he brushed off his hands on his beer belly, covered by a white T-shirt, causing a puff of flour.

"Yeah, Tom is our postman, too," Mike answered.

"Paul Walker used to mow his lawn but since he went off to college he uses some commercial lawn service he hired on the Internet." Mr. Delio sounded kind of worried.

"Anything odd, come straight to me." Mr. Delio placed a hand on his shoulder. It felt like a ritual, a sacred trust. "Oh, and the book thing is not odd. Normal. He just reads a lot."

Doctor Clark Loved Pizza

Mike pulled his 1970 Dodge Dart into the driveway of Dr. Clark's house at 5:15pm. It was a tidy-looking ranch style house. The lawn was mowed. The trees and shrubs pruned. The beds were all edged and mulched. In back he could see from the cement driveway that there was a detached, closed up, two car garage.

There was an old Chevy van in the driveway. The tags were expired.

Mike climbed out with the insulated pizza cover and the six-pack of Mountain Dew. He climbed the three steps up to the covered porch. Directly to the left was a large trash barrel that was nicely concealed from the street by the tall hedge that surrounded the porch.

There was no storm door or screen door. He paused and looked at the laminated card once more. He knocked and tried the handle. It was not locked.

He opened it and walked in. He was so taken aback by what he saw that he almost forgot to announce himself. "Delio's Pizza."

He was standing in a foyer. A hallway went straight back to the kitchen. An arch to his immediate left went into what was usually a living room, dining room combination. The layout of the building was normal. Mike had been in many homes that were made the same all over town.

The odd thing was that every wall was lined with bookcases. Every one of them was completely full. Where there was not a bookcase, books were in piles that went just as high. Bookcases were even in front of the windows. This made the rooms dark, except there were desk lamps all along the top shelves. These were the classic kind with the green shades.

As he moved down the hallway, it felt constricted by the books crowding each side, making the hall narrow. Before entering the kitchen, the hall to the back bedrooms opened on his right side. It was also lined with books.

Not watching where he was going, the large pizza box insulator toppled a tower of books just as he entered the kitchen, causing a small, mostly quiet avalanche. Trying to stop it only seemed to make it worse. He stepped aside quickly and set the pizza and sodas on the island in the kitchen, next to the prior insulated pizza delivery container. This was a detail not on the card but Mr. Delio had remembered to tell him to leave the whole thing and take the other back.

The kitchen was full of books as well. The kitchen table was completely covered in a mountain of books that was higher than Mike's head. All but one of the kitchen cabinet doors had been removed and books piled inside. The lone cabinet door was directly to the right of where the stove would be if it had been there. In the gap of the counters where the stove would normally be was a large wheeled trash barrel exactly like the one on the porch.

Mike opened the fridge and just as described there was a $20 bill on the empty top shelf. He replaced it with the Mountain Dew.

The next shelf had two cardboard flats that were cases of some kind of protein drink called Ensure. One case had been partially used. The door had only a large bottle of Centrum Silver multi-vitamins. He had never heard of the brand.

For some reason, he looked in the freezer. It needed defrosting. A single frozen dinner was slowly being consumed by the frost glacier.

He closed it and folded the $20 bill and put it in the same shirt pocket as the laminated card.

He reached over to lift the lid of the trash barrel to peek inside as he wondered if this was the trash can mentioned or was it the other. Or both.

Mike saw a Delio's pizza box was mostly covered with other smaller boxes with the word Amazon in the trash can. The kind of boxes books were delivered with. For some reason he counted the nine Amazon boxes. There were nine since his last pizza. The trash barrel was only half full so he left it, wondering if it would fit down the narrow hall.

He had not heard a sound as he started back out. His mission was accomplished.

Slowly he moved back down the narrow hall and this time he was looking at the book titles as he went. There was a lot of science fiction. It made Mike smile. Mixed in were text books on a huge number of topics like quantum physics, computer science, psychology, philosophy, chemistry, biology and even hydroponics. That was just a glancing sample.

"Thanks, Dave." Mike heard a voice call out from the back bedrooms.

"You're welcome, Dr. Clark," was his reply as he moved more quickly to the door.

On the porch, the trash barrel was empty. Mike climbed in his car and headed back to Delio's.

)))) ● ● ● ● ● ● ((((

The rest of the summer was much the same. There were deliveries twice a week. Every two weeks he would switch out the trash barrel. He later discovered that Tom the postman would return the empty can to the porch after pickup.

Mike actually saw Dr. Clark only once that summer. It was a chance encounter as he was leaving and Dr. Clark was exiting the bathroom. He saw Mike and waved, saying, "Thanks, Dave. Say Hi to your papa for me."

"Will do." Mike said and moved along.

Doctor Clark Loved Pizza

It was October; just after Columbus Day, when Tom Wilkins stopped in at Delio's to pick up a pizza for his own family on the way home from work. He was still in his postman uniform. Mike was at the counter taking orders that day.

"Hi, Mr. Wilkins, what can we get you today?" Mike smiled, thinking he and Tom were kind of a team. Wilkins must have been thinking the same thing.

"Mike. Please. Call me Tom." Tom looked around to see if anyone was else was there. No one was. "How does he seem to you?"

"Um, the same. I never really interact with Dr. Clark. It's just the usual. Why?" Mike was curious at Tom's tone.

"He seemed agitated in the last few weeks." Tom said flatly. He was obviously worried. Mike said nothing, allowing Tom to continue. The silence encouraged him.

"He gets a lot of deliveries. The UPS and FedEx guys change all the time and they just drop the packages on the doormat and ring the doorbell. Dr. Clark never sees the packages. So I pretend to deliver them. I pretend he has to sign for everything, too. Even the stuff he doesn't have to sign for. It's how I check on him. Know what I mean."

Mike nodded. The door opened and a Mrs. Cook came in for a pickup with two-year-old Jennifer on her hip. She said hi to Tom briefly as Mike rung her up. Tom stepped back as if he was waiting for his order.

When she was gone, Tom leaned forward again. "All that stuff I deliver. Not just books. Parts of stuff. Some packages have hazmat codes and shit."

"What can I do?" Mike asked.

"Today there was a kind of a sound in there. A rumble." He wiped his face, "I could feel it in the sidewalk for the whole block."

"As far as I can tell all he does is read in there," Mike said. "I don't see how he would have time for anything else. You see how many books he gets delivered."

"Just keep an eye on him." Tom closed the conversation. "If you can."

Mike was trying not to worry about Dr. Clark. Mike was just the pizza delivery guy. What was an 18-year-old kid supposed to do anyway? Dr. Clark was an adult. He had pizza on Mondays and Thursdays like clockwork and he left the best tips of the week.

Mike smiled. Today was Thursday.

Mike pulled in Dr. Clark's driveway and ran up to the door, barely pausing to knock.

"Delio's Pizza!" he called out and proceeded directly back to the kitchen, as always.

DOCTOR CLARK LOVED PIZZA

Mike was startled by Dr. Clark standing on the opposite side of the kitchen island. The single cabinet with a door on it was open behind him and he was reading an open book on the island counter as he ate a strawberry Pop-Tart.

Mike knew it was a staple item for Dr. Clark. Every week or so there was an empty Pop-Tart box in the trash. Mike felt nosey for knowing that.

Dr. Clark glanced up from the novel he was reading briefly, lifting it from the island. It looked to be another sci-fi novel titled *Still Falling*. He raised his half-eaten Pop-Tart in a toast like gesture saying, "Oh… Hi David."

"Hi, Dr. Clark." Mike quickly switched the pizza warmers and placed the Mountain Dew in the fridge, snagging the $20. When he turned back, Dr. Clark was staring at him. It was the first real good look Mike had of the man. He was younger than Mike originally thought, maybe 50 years old. His graying hair was combed back from his bearded face into a thick pony tail.

"What time is it?" Dr. Clark asked.

"5:25pm, sir. Sorry to be a little late." Mike looked at his Pop-Tart.

"Is it Monday?" Dr. Clark looked out the window, puzzled.

"No, sir. It's Thursday." Mike replied. Dr. Clark had on a fresh Oxford shirt. It was untucked over jeans. The laundry tag was still in the button hole.

"You are not David Delio," he stated.

"No, sir." Mike tried to keep it simple.

Dr. Clark closed his book on his finger and walked past Mike saying, "Thank you, Not David Delio." He disappeared into the back of the house. Before Mike reached the front door, he felt it, more than heard it. There was a hum of some great device and a change of pressure in the air.

A week later, he knocked and entered as usual. Even before he reached the kitchen he had an odd feeling the house was empty. There was no hum, no creak of floorboards, and no sense of life that he had always felt before.

Mike's unease grew when he entered the kitchen and saw that all the books that had been on the kitchen table had been simply pushed off the far side of the table and left there in a great tumbled pile on the floor beyond the table. He kept staring at the pile as he traded pizza warmers, tucking the now flapping empty one under his arm and set the Mountain Dew in the fridge and collected his $20.

All the cans of Ensure were gone. So were the vitamins.

Following habit, he turned to check the trash and saw the single cabinet door was open to reveal completely empty shelves.

He froze when he opened the trash barrel lid.

Doctor Clark Loved Pizza

He had become used to the contents of this trash can. Pizza boxes, Pop-Tart wrappers and boxes, empty drink cans and Amazon shipping boxes. This time he saw a couple dozen empty ammunition boxes. Half were labeled Remington Subsonic 9mm, the other half were labeled Remington .223 and looked like rifle ammunition, based on the cover photo.

Mike quietly let the trash can cover close.

Softly he moved to the hall that went back to the bedrooms. The lights were off there in the hall. How long had they been off? How many times had he simply walked in and out, not noticing a thing? Mike stopped at the end of the hall. It suddenly raised the hair on his neck like it was a gaping maw.

"Hello… Dr. Clark?" Mike waited and the longer he waited the more courage bled from him. "Dr. Clark? Is everything OK? It's me, Not David Delio. Remember?"

He stepped into the hall.

"My name is actually Mike. I should have told you before." Mike said to the air as he saw the hall bath door open. He turned on the light. It let precious little illumination into the hall. The bathroom was very clean in there. Surprisingly there was only one book inside. It seemed so odd that he craned his neck to see the title, *Temporal Displacement: A String Theory Approach.*

The first door on the right was closed. He called out as he turned the knob. There was only one light inside and it was a floor lamp next to a reading chair. The room was lined with filled book cases. Folding tables had been set up in front of them on two sides in the shape of an L and mountains of books were just piled there. Most were dusty and cobwebbed. No pretense of order here. Books were read and just added to the pile.

The next room on the right was much the same, but worse. "Dr. Clark?" That room had been filled to shoulder height with books and forgotten, hoarder fashion. The door was difficult to push open due to some prior small avalanche.

The last door made Mike afraid. Visions of finding Dr. Clark's dead body filled Mikes head like the books of that last room.

"Dr. Clark? Pizza guy's here." The door swung open easily to an empty room.

It was intended to be the master bedroom. It was now a high-tech workshop of some kind. The walls were lined with work benches that were covered with a variety of equipment and tools. Mike recognized several computer brand names, there were many monitors on one wall, including a dominant 40-inch-high def monitor in the center of the cluster of dark screens. There was only one keyboard and mouse.

The master bathroom had even become part of the shop. The shower had been converted to some kind of emergency chemical wash down booth. A stainless-steel counter replaced the vanity and toilet. More unusual tools and equipment covered the surfaces.

The only other door in the room was for the walk-in closet. It had clothes in it. They were on the back most wall only. All the shirts, pants and even boxers were in dry cleaning bags. They were another familiar trash item. There was also a narrow cot in the closet with a single pillow, plus disheveled blankets and sheets.

Dr. Clark wasn't here. Mike's relief was quickly replaced with the feeling he was invading Dr. Clark's personal spaces. Embarrassed, Mike closed the door and fled the house.

The following Monday he returned, not knowing what to expect.

He didn't expect music. Or laughter.

"Delio's Pizza!" Mike called out as he entered. As he stepped into the kitchen, Dr. Clark came in right behind him. He took the pizza right from Mike's hands, leaving him holding the insulated carrier.

"Thank you, Not David Delio." He smiled as he dropped it on the kitchen table, tossed open the lid and tore into the pie like a ravenous wolf. Led Zeppelin was still playing from the back.

Before Mike could put the Mountain Dew in the fridge, Clark snagged two of them, which allowed Mike to look closer at him before saying, "Are you all right, sir? Can I get you anything?" His clothes were dirty and threadbare.

The question made Dr. Clark laugh. The man looked thinner since Thursday. His hair seemed much longer, his beard was even grayer. *How could that be?*

"These are wonderful times, my boy. Enjoy them." He raised his Mountain Dew like the finest champagne, in a toast. "Here is to… so much fresh water that we shit in it!" He laughed and drained his Mountain Dew.

"Oh, by the way, tell Delio he can keep the balance of my pizza advance." He grabbed another piece of pizza as he got up and walked to a kitchen drawer. From it he came out with a nearly full bundle of $20 bills and another of $100 bills.

"This is for you, son." He held it out until Mike took it. "Invest it in Microsoft, Cisco and Hagan Enterprises. Trust me." He laughed again and stuffed too much pizza in his mouth as he closed the box. He grabbed the other Mountain Dew and the pizza and without another word, went to the back room.

Mike was in shock as he quietly left the house. Dr. Clark continued to laugh while he listened to "Stairway to Heaven". Before Mike even reached his car he heard that hum, felt it in his bones through his feet, the rumble and pressure felt in his ears was building.

And then it was like someone slammed a door on it. The sound was gone.

Mike got in his car and pulled away. He didn't see any smoke from the fire as he drove away. It was slow to start, they said later. So much paper made for a spectacular fire. The clouds above had glowed from the towering light of it.

* * *

"There were no signs of any remains ever found," Tom Wilkins said to Mike a week later as they looked into the blackened crater of a foundation. "It's not unheard-of for a fire like that."

Mike smiled, remembering his laughter. He remembered the equipment, the book titles of first editions that were like new. "He'll be back. Dr. Clark sure loved pizza…"

Two

Money Tree

S.C. Megale

S.C. Megale, known to the pigeons she feeds as Shea, was born in 1995 in Reston, Virginia. She is the author of more than two dozen YA manuscripts, and her first published novel, *This is Not a Love Scene,* released with St. Martin's Press/Wednesday Books in 2019. She's taught writing workshops at both schools and libraries nationwide and is an English tutor. Apart from writing, she is passionate about wildlife, history, and humanity

Money Tree

In this next selection Shea describes an alien world complete with whimsical inhabitants in an exotic environment. But even here, there is a quiet economy at play. If the love of money is the root of all evil, what is at the root of the *Money Tree*?

This is dedicated to the Hourlings,
who I love with all my heart.

And to that one time Bill A. looked up
from his laptop and said "YOU FOOLS!"

Fingers snapped loud and fast next to my face.

I looked up from the adze in my palms and Tekwani swatted me on the back of the head.

His chestnut eyes rolled in their crazy way like eggs in a greased bowl, chastising me. A scarf of hard, hairy ruberry shells fell down either side of his broad shoulders and a white monkey's tail looped around his waist. At my feet were the dregs of dried, tan money leaves used to giftwrap the adze. My silence, I guess, was uncordial, and Tekwani tilted his black-haired head and jabbed a finger at the woman sitting at the bench across from me. Clicking noises of firm expectation came from his throat.

I sighed and turned to look at the plump woman whose face was so etched with wrinkles and framed with fluffy shawls that I couldn't see which of the lines were her eyes; her cheeks pushed so hard against them with a smile. Her fingers steepled together in a hopeful way, awaiting my positive reception of her gift.

I lifted the adze – a simple flat sloth's nail attached to a simple straight stick, available for free at any splitting room, even to young girls like me – to my forehead and bowed three times. The old woman laughed and clapped.

I pursed my lips and rotated my eyes to Tekwani. He raised his chin approvingly and those wild eyes continued to stir like weathervanes in a storm, but the corners of his lips inclined.

Sweet sap perfumed the air and fogged the insides of my nose. The Money Tree was bleeding its juices around the bark today and coating it with a gleam. A release of ruberry pods would be tumbling their way down its towering branches soon to nourish us. The carved interior walls were honey-colored and seats and arches were riddled right into the soft flesh of the titanic organism. We bobbed on floorboards also fashioned from the branches. The Money Tree allowed the lightning spirits to sever from him anything we needed.

The old woman across from me shifted in her seat to watch the next third-generation open his gift. Identical to mine. All of us, boy and girl, were turning fourteen today, and the Great Barrenness had already settled upon the women as the prophecy said. Personally, I had never bled. No more children would be birthed to the Money Tree. One day soon, the Money

Tree will reward us with the Eternal Harvest – fruit that will last us forever.

Hmph. My stomach twisted.

I slapped my knee and raised my eyebrows at Tekwani. *Can we go now?*

Tekwani gnawed his lip with pointy yellow teeth and spun his eyes and wiggled his brow again.

Mmmm okay, Mayana. Let's put that adze to use!

Tekwani grinned with an open mouth.

He led me out of the thick humidity that came with dwelling inside a living thing. Outside the trunk of the Money Tree we walked around terraces with rails and ropes cascading down from the braided branches to keep us aloft. Below, the ground was invisible. Above, unthinkable. All to be seen were the knots and tangles of the Money Tree's prism, like being inside a woven basket. Lime-green, long, floppy leaves of the Tree sprouted between the smooth beige branches.

The air was looser out here. Heat still rubbed our skin as we moved through it. Tekwani pulled off his organic, stitched shirt and let the ruberry pod scarf rattle into his large hand. Like all of us, his skin was the brownish color of soaked reeds and had a rough, hemp-like texture. He was a second-generation, in his late thirties. He was my Twig – my guardian, companion, but not my father, decided upon by the shamans of the Money Tree. Parents were irrelevant with the revolving of procreators every fourteen to twenty years. I did not desire to know mine.

What I did desire was to have a different reaction to what Tekwani just said with quick, playful shakes of his hand at the side of his head.

That adze will split juice all over your lap…

A bitter shudder of distaste itched in my blood.

Most in the tribe flooded with saliva at the thought of the slimy, lavender guts of the ruberry pods. It sat like paste on my tongue, though, and went down like iron. Nothing energized, satisfied, and quelled more than its sustenance, but my stomach always trembled and my tonsils were scalded with bile at the thought of every meal.

Everyone dreamt of the promised Eternal Harvest. We could live in happiness without the constant labor of collecting its fruit, splitting open the pods, distributing its tangy innards, and collecting it all over again.

And then everyone would stop scavenging for more food – birds, monkeys, nuts – and gorge contentedly on their favorite ruberry while I scraped the remnants off my tastebuds with a dead beetle just to mask the flavor. Forced to consume it and quiet my hunger.

Tekwani and I stomped up the terrace stairs in a circular fashion, around and around the tree trunk. I couldn't help but follow the curl and calligraphy of the black tattoo that climbed across the muscles of his back.

Three sires of men will work with the Tree
Placed here for ripening by the Gods That Be™
When the pods they shall split are all empty inside

Money Tree

Then gather each adze for the ultimate bide
With the Money Tree's nutrition the humans will keep
Until the Eternal Harvest where all will be reaped.

I couldn't imagine the thunder of *all* the pods of the Money Tree raining down upon us. Any day now that could happen and I would freeze wherever I was and listen while others ran to the splitting rooms to receive. Would I abandon the tribe then? Would I arrange a coalition to continue hunting for different food anyway? Would I accept gulping down a putrid shiver at every supper?

Thump!

Thump!

Thwack!

We entered the round splitting room. Gutters filtered in from the ceiling and the large, hairy pods spilled off them and into trellises. First, second, and third generations – old and young – stood in a circle grasping tools, waiting for all of the pods to rumble down before going to open them. Barrels of adzes flanked all three entrances into the room, and I cast an annoyed eye at it. The shaman-woman most likely got her bulk bargain gifts from here.

I crossed my arms and held my own adze lazily. I tried not to glare at the accumulating orbs of ruberry in the trellises. No one knew of my distaste. Not even Tekwani.

One last pod bumped down into the pile and silence stretched. At last, everyone drew forward and shoveled pods into their arms or shirts. I clumped together an armful, hobbled to the center of the room, and let them shower to the floor, crouching after them. In unison with everyone else, I raised my tool and thwacked it into the shell. A creamy, light-purple seam met the edge of my blade. I turned the pod and whacked into it again.

One by one, and then all together, like a rainstorm slowly beginning, halves of shells fell apart to the floor at the impact of an adze.

And then stopped.

Completely.

No one moved. No one breathed.

I let spit pool in my mouth and drown my teeth because I feared swallowing would recall the taste again.

Every single pod was bare inside.

The prophecy had begun.

› › › • • • • • • • ‹ ‹ ‹

Hollers pierced my ears and dancing wobbled the planks at my feet. I swept my few belongings – hardened sap earrings, water jug still swirling with termites, salve, slingshot, and clothes – into a sack and slung it over my shoulders. Smoke threaded incense into my nostrils and made me cough as I spun for the door letting out of the Money Tree interior.

Tekwani stood at the threshold, where the prophecy's words were carved again around the doorframe. For once his face was stripped of humor, scarred mouth in a deep frown.

I came up to him and braced his forearms.

You were a good Twig.

Tekwani flicked my ear and scowled again. I exhaled and looked down, tottering my head side to side.

It would take long to explain, I expressed.

My stomach growled. I went on.

I am leaving now.

Tekwani tilted his head. His dark eyes still bounced around, but they looked genuinely sad.

I had to shoulder past him.

Singing beat together rhythms as the entire tribe crowded in the highest splitting room of the Money Tree, raising their hands to the heavenly canopy to receive their eternal reward. I couldn't raise my eyes to it.

I swung myself over the railing of the outer terrace and hugged the twirly branches of the tree. It was smooth enough to slide down with my legs snug around it, and when I hit an intercourse or a knob, I shimmied.

Food was more important than family.

About thirty meters down, that is when I heard the roar.

I froze and clutched the trunk.

Below, I could feel something bite into the base of the Money Tree. The entire trunk swayed.

Sawdust billowed into the air. Clouds of some other fume – silvery and sharp-smelling – collided with it. I closed my eyes tight in fear and then –

When another set of jaws plunged into the base of the tree, I lost my grasp. I was jutted off the trunk and somersaulted through air towards the ground.

A net of vines and foliage saved my life. I *oophed!* as leaves shook into my eyes and pain twisted my ankle. But already my hand was swiping away the brush to see what monster those roaring and biting and bad-breath-emitting jaws belonged to.

The creature was big, metallic, and white, with pincers at its front that plowed into the gigantic wood base and made mulch out of the Money Tree's skin. It had strange, rubbery round wheels for legs.

On its side was another tattoo in huge, inviting letters.

THE GODS THAT BE™
FARMING FRESH HUMANS
SINCE '93!

Panicky chirps croaked from my throat as I stared hard at the tattoos.

That's when I saw black, furry claws gripping levers and handles inside the big white monster, operating it…

Tekwani! I needed to warn him! We had it all wrong! I needed to –!

Something big and heavy and fleshy fell into the vine net next to me, making us rock and creak and shuffle. I jerked over, heart spiking, afraid it was one of those black furry aliens inside the white monster.

Instead, a human finger flicked my temple lovingly.

Twig! I beamed. *You came after me!*

Sapling! You came before me! Tekwani crawled out of the bushy foliage towards me. *We must get you back to –*

I clamped my palm over his grunting mouth and turned his face firmly towards the monster. His manic eyes ricocheted off them and onto me and back again.

The roar of their jaws turned into a deafening screech. Nearly half of the Money Tree was eaten at the base…it began to lean…

And that was that. I clasped Tekwani's hand, towed him from the netting, and made him run with me.

Away. Until the roars would become echoes.

I felt sad for our tribe. But I understood the passion of having to love what you eat.

I squeezed Tekwani's wrist tight as the colossal crash of the Money Tree shook the entire forest around us.

My harvester adze poked into my back from the pack that hung from me. But I'd have to stop calling it that. Because now I know.

We're not the farmers.

We're the fruit.

THREE

A WORLD WITHOUT TAXI DRIVERS

NATHAN LAZARUS

Nathan Lazarus is an engineer and long-time fan of science fiction. He has recently been writing short fiction in preparation for starting work on his first novel.

In this next piece, Nathan takes us on a scenic trip in the back of a taxi. Our tour is narrated by a spirited driver who describes the future history of conflict between corporations and the working man. The trick, of course, as with any conflict, is to know which side you're on. Something to think about, as the meter begins to run.

You look like a man who needs a ride. Not the sort who'd settle for one of those cheap autocars, not a gentleman like you. With that tailored suit, those cufflinks, the watch subtle enough to be worth a fortune, I can tell you have refined taste. Tough to find a real taxi driver these days, a real *human* taxi driver. Well, today's your lucky day. You're looking at Charlie Edwards, tour guide extraordinaire, and I must say the best taxi driver west of the Mississippi. Perhaps the only taxi driver this side of the Mississippi, since Wilson down in Sunnyvale turned in his license last month. I see you're sold: who could pass up an opportunity to ride with an institution? Good, good, let me grab your bags. Why don't you take a seat, anywhere you'd like. Just vacuumed this morning. Another thing you don't get with those damn robots; I take pride in my car, always have, always will. Not a scratch in the paint, not a dent in the fender; you'd never know it came off the assembly line more than ten years ago. When you're in Charlie's hands, you will get where you're going, and you'll do it in style.

What brings you to our fine city? No, no, let me guess. When you've been around as long as I have, you can tell a few things. No skis, could hardly be a tourist around these parts. Not with those beautiful slopes outside of town, with four inches of clean new snow falling yesterday. You can't be visiting friends or family; wouldn't need a taxi driver, eh? It must be business, and with clothes like that I can tell business is good. And not enough luggage to be setting up shop… you must be here for a conference. A robotics trade show? Well, close enough. The Valley Estate Hotel it is, and what a drive it'll be. Now there are those who might take Highway 39, but any driver worth his medallion knows that's bumper to bumper on an afternoon like this one. Nah, we're going to take a different route, down some hidden byways and back streets that'll get you there in half the time. Great scenery, the best parts of town, and a beautiful day for it. Makes you wonder about the folks who'd rather be driven by one of those computerized monstrosities to save a few bucks. Can you imagine getting a tour from your local Roomba?

It's not often I run into a roboticist like yourself, one of the enemy. Now now, don't look so concerned, I'm just messing with you. This is the town for a fella like you. Can't go more than a few hundred feet around here without hammering full tilt into a milestone of cybernetics. Just take a look out the window there. The townhall building. A pristine example of the mid-twentieth century modernist architectural style pioneered by the architect La Corbusier, as our tourism bureau would say. A concrete bunker better suited for Normandy beach, as I call it. Brutalism at its worst. I've always had a fondness for it myself. Deep beneath that ugly façade beats the heart of a metropolis, from the mayor to the street cleaning brigade. See the corner window with the light on, on the third floor? *The* Ellroy Benningham got his start right there. That's right: el Presidente himself. You should have seen him back then. Those bright orange suspenders could blind you all the way up 16th street. A spitting image of my great uncle Lars. Back before the image consultants got a hold of poor Elroy, of course. I believed in him. That "hero of the working man" routine. We all did. And he did right by us. It was here that we made history. The first city in America to ban AI from our streets. I can tell you right here and now, I cried like a baby that day. You could see his John Hancock all the way from the moon. The greatest day of my life. I knew, then and there, that those damn microchips, those chunks of silicon, were not going to take away the job of this here cabby. No sir, not me.

You look like a bright young man. Let's see if you can take a guess at this next one, just around the corner. A simple, elegant sculpture, done in the finest polished brass, with the words "August 30th, 2052: we remember." Not a clue? What are they teaching you young people in history class these days? This spot, 7th and Water Street, is where it all started to come down. A simple traffic accident, nothing more. A tractor trailer makes a wide left, and bang, one overeager commuter converted into blood and scrap metal. Happens all the time. Didn't rate a mention in the local newspaper. How it would have been different if that commuter hadn't had the name "Benningham." Course, it was all a sham. Why, everybody who was anybody knew Ellroy detested, DETESTED, that spendthrift nephew of his. Hadn't spoken in over a decade, I hear. But a "consultant," you know, one of those talking heads, caught his ear. AI was the future. That whole anti-automation thing, it's a midterm loser out in Maine and the Sun Belt. What a crock. Why, those types, with their fancy degrees and tailored suits, they don't know the first thing about human nature. Present company excluded, I'm sure. You shoulda seen him three weeks later. That trembling voice. Breaking with emotion at all the right moments. Every middle-class soccer mom in the country swooned. We could yell until we were blue in the face that a skilled driver was no more dangerous than a robo-car. But it was too late. A single grieving uncle was worth a thousand of those damn risk assessment studies. It was to be those self-driving cars, or safeguards that cost ten times as much.

One day, on top of the world, not a cloud on the horizon. The next, so far underwater that I had to go up to the top of Mount Wilkins to breathe. When the union boys came with their delusional visions, it is any wonder that I bought them wholesale? And they had a plan: on April 23, 2054, 25 years to the day after the founding of Randall Robotics, the mother of them all, we took to the streets. It was here, on Harbor Drive, that it began. Call it what you will, the Platinum Mile, Billionaire's Row, the Yellow Brick Road, this stretch is our city's beating heart of commerce. On 6 AM the morning of the 23rd, it stopped. Wall to wall taxi cabs on every exit, placards at every storefront. The first commuters heading into the city were welcomed by a mob of angry drivers. It wasn't long before they gave up and headed home. One look in our eyes told them we were here to stay. When those big businessmen looked out from their penthouses all they could see were the millions bleeding onto the streets. I knew they'd cave, and cave they did. But they had one last card to play: Elroy Benningham himself.

Our final tour stop, you'll recognize. Why, I bet it's on your trade show pamphlet. Randall Robotics Headquarters, anchor of Billionaire's Row. The site of both our greatest victory and our greatest defeat. The corks started popping as soon as the presidential motorcade began inching down the waterfront. You shoulda seen me and the boys, coated in dirt and bandages beside those sharp dressing lawyers. Ol' Elroy played his part to the hilt. Sure, he was "impartial." All he wanted was to clear up this little misunderstanding. That smile of his, that firm handshake, dripped with sincerity. Even the orange suspenders were back to remind us of the good old days. The final surrender took less than two hours. Our leader read the terms, only two sentences long, from the Randall HQ balcony: "No vehicle may be driven autonomously by an integrated computer system under any circumstances. Any method of control, human or otherwise, must use the steering wheel, ignition and foot pedals." I celebrated as loudly as anyone that day. We'd gotten everything we had hoped for, and more.

I was right here on the Stephen's Gorge Bridge two weeks later when the full betrayal became apparent. It came blaring out of the radio in a special bulletin: "Randall Robotics announces the humanoid Model Y-37: Next Generation Vehicle Control System. Includes state-of-the-art personality routines!" My cell phone rang the whole way back to the garage, be greeted with the lights of a hundred cop cars. The president was taking no chances. It has gone down in history as Black Tuesday: every protest leader was brought in that morning, with charges ranging from "Failure to disperse" to "First degree murder." I was one of the lucky ones, minor enough to be left with a six-month suspended sentence. The ringleaders got almost thirty years. From then on, it was a matter of time. I knew that evening that the sun was setting on the era of the cabbie.

Here we are: 980 Pine, the Valley Estate Hotel. Five star accommodations with rooftop bar and restaurant, and walking distance from the Park of the Modern Ancients and the Museums of Lower Midtown. Let me help you with your bags. Looks like your fare is 34 dollars and 15 cents. Why thank you, that's very generous. Take care now, it's been a pleasure. And good luck with your trade fair. Here's my card. Feel free to give me a call when you need a ride back to the airport.

PERSONALITY ROUTINE 3
BITTER CAB DRIVER... TERMINATED

Y 37 PASSENGER SEARCH ROUTINE INITIATED...
PASSENGER IDENTIFIED
COMMENCING HOSPITALITY ROUTINE...

You look like a man who needs a ride. Not the sort who'd settle for one of those cheap autocars, not a gentleman like you…

FOUR

IMAGINE GIANTS

SUSAN SAYLER

Susan Sayler is a futurist with a degree in the humanities. She is fascinated by trans-humanism and the ways that applied science will broaden the capacities of the human race. Susan's writing is often a marriage of the transformative power of technology and the tender touch of the human condition. Susan's blog is called *The Future Global Universe* **globalempress.blogspot.com**.

Back from the moon, Neil Armstrong said "*I put up my thumb and blotted out the planet Earth. I didn't feel like a giant. I felt very, very small.*" Susan's story explores that idea through the eyes of two little boys, brothers, experimenting with the world, you might say. And her writing unearths some wonderful questions. Einstein said "*To raise new questions requires creative imagination and marks real advance.*" I suspect he would have loved Susan's work.

Ouch!" JasperR9049 instinctively put his finger in his mouth, seeing the bright yellow-gold blood oozing from the tiny puncture wound on the tip of his middle finger. The puncture was caused by a fishing hook while he was sorting through his dad's tackle box, looking to borrow his nifty new monofilament crawlers.

Movement caught his eye and looking up, he saw his brother, MalcomR9049 through the garage window. Malcolm was heading into his makeshift laboratory in a room attached to the garage used to be a storage room.

Jasper grabbed the crawlers he wanted and some other stuff from the box and then quickly headed over to see if Malcolm wanted to go fishing with him before Malcolm got too absorbed in one of his experiments.

"What are you doing now?" Jasper asked Malcolm as he entered the lab. It wasn't asked in a language that any human might have known. No human being would even be able to hear this voice.

"I am going to prove to you that I am right! There is an entire civilization of life forms living on this one cell. They live in houses and they communicate with one another." Malcolm answered, adjusting the microscope and working the lighting to minimize the glare on his lens. "My new algorithms are blowing my mind. The program combines motion, light, sound and heat to create a picture of what is going on in this new nano-world that I germinated. Freakin' amazing!"

"You told me an hour ago they were fish. Make up your mind." Jasper yawned.

"They were, now they have evolved." Malcolm replied while writing numbers on a spreadsheet, adjusting a lens again, and then turning several dials on his elaborate computer system.

"It's amazing how much time you are willing to waste on this nonsense. Nano-germs that have language? And they even use computers? Bacteria that have artificial intelligence? You should write comic books, Mal," Jasper said.

Malcolm was a budding young scientist destined for great things; of that, everyone was absolutely certain. In this latest discovery, he had created a world of living entities that were possibly just as intelligent as his own civilization. But that was not the big deal. What was truly extraordinary was that his software was able to watch the evolution of their culture unfold. This was going to get him a huge award at the university. His professor was going be stoked. The greatest scholars alive would applaud his discovery.

Nonetheless, glory and fame were not what really mattered to Malcolm. His passion for science was more akin to an obsession. He compulsively searched for answers and he especially loved to study evolution.

Jasper gave in, downplaying his growing interest. "Okay, I guess you are not going to go down to the lake with me today. Go ahead; show me what you are talking about."

Jasper took off his jacket and sat at the workstation next to his brother, as he had done so many times in the past. "What are we doing here?"

"See these life forms on the screen? They are living on this Earth cell I germinated last night." Malcolm shifted the monitor so Jasper could get a good view.

Malcolm continued, "These life forms are extremely small and their time reference is also microscopic."

"Okay, I see," his brother said. Jasper was also pretty astute when it came to science.

"Now realize that due to the difference in size, time passes in our world a lot slower than in their world. What would be two billion years to them is only a few hours to us," Malcolm added.

"Yeah, so what?"

"So, check this out. I started them out on the Earth cell as single particles. Now watch, in just a few minutes, they evolve into fish!"

"Cool, I can see them changing. How did you do that?"

Malcolm ignored his brother's question, concentrating on his project. "Now watch, they start changing into reptiles and, get this, they start having sexual reproduction!"

"Get out! Let me see that."

"See? All kinds of them have lost the gills and developed scales. And in just a few more minutes, now look; a lot of them develop wings and start flying around."

"Fucking blow me away. I see what you mean. Some are actually flying around like birds now!"

"And, you haven't seen anything yet. Watch."

Both young men sat staring into the computer monitor, Malcolm tapping his foot impatiently. Jasper's jaw dropped open in rapt fascination.

"Looks like they are multiplying at a rapid rate," Jasper commented after a few minutes.

Malcolm adjusted the instruments and played with a few more dials on his computer system.

"Okay, there it is. There are all kinds of mammals now. See? They have legs. I know if we had instruments to measure it, I could prove they have become warm-blooded mammals at this point."

"Damn, this is getting creepy," Jasper exclaimed.

"It gets creepier. Hominids, like apes and monkeys, appear in just about a half hour from now. Then some of those lose all their fur and start making their own clothes and shit. Hard to tell how they do it, we can't see it all that well, but we know they have a layer over their bodies of material that they construct themselves," Malcolm said.

"So, what happens in an hour from now?" asked Jasper.

"Yeah, that is the part that sucks. We have to kill them all off and start over, because they overpopulate so rapidly, it would kill the Earth cell if I let them continue. We don't have enough Earth cells to waste on these experiments."

"Damn, that sucks royal," said Jasper.

"I have talked with my professor, though, and we are looking for ways to curtail their breeding. No doubt the human culture would diverge into a dead-end strictly human group and a more promising trans-human group."

"Make them all homosexual!" Jasper suggested.

Malcolm rolled his eyes. "Right," he said, sarcastically.

"You are going to get a full scholarship for this one, bro," Jasper said, truly impressed now.

"I hope so. If we are successful, then we will be able to see how they evolve past the human phase. My guess is that after the human phase they lose a lot of biological parts in favor of digital parts because digital things take less energy to maintain and afford a lot more flexibility and expansion."

"You mean they become more like us, right?" asked Jasper. "Hmmm, do you think they will eventually develop some kind of master artificial general intelligence?"

"I am almost sure of it," answered Malcolm, nodding his head.

"Hey bro, I am just wondering. Do you think that could be dangerous? Could they figure out a way to infect our systems with something deadly?" Jasper shivered.

"Well, we are not letting this cell out of the lab, for sure. We aren't going to take any chances," Malcolm reassured him.

"It's like they evolve the same way we do, but they are nano size and they don't even know we exist. They have no idea that we are watching them," Jasper surmised.

"Yeah, makes you wonder if there is some giant entity watching us right now, huh?" Malcolm chuckled.

"Don't be ridiculous, Mal. Come on, let's go fishing."

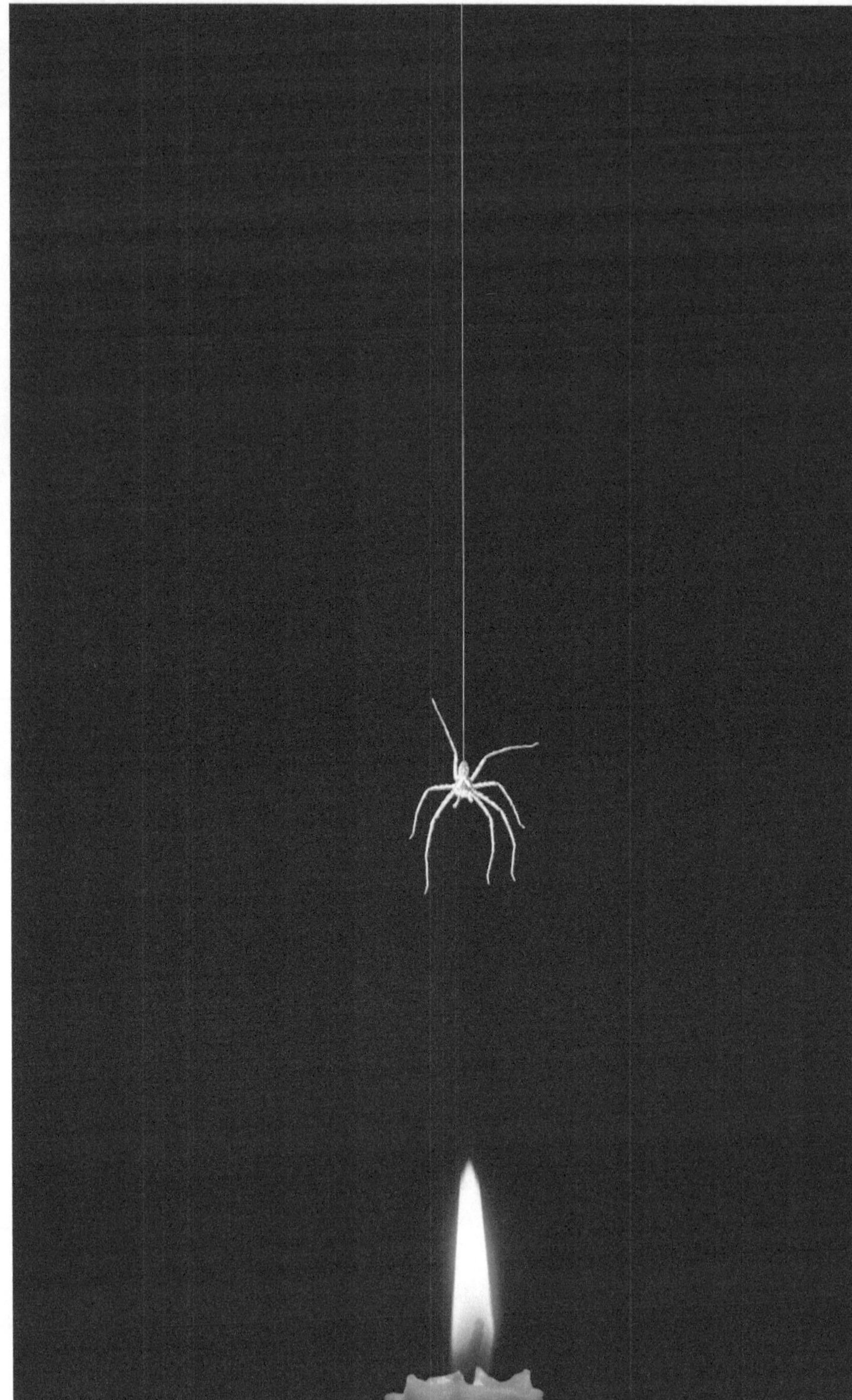

FIVE

MAGIC ACT

BILL KRIEGER

Bill Krieger is a Madison Avenue creative director and copywriter who is a native son of the Bronx. He's best known for his award-winning advertising for HBO and Time Warner. His prose also raises millions of dollars each year for great causes such as Amnesty International, NARAL Pro-Choice America, Habitat for Humanity and other essential nonprofits. He has won over 45 writing awards across all media, including TV and radio. If you enjoy this story, tell him so at: **Krieger.BillKrieger@gmail.com**.

Shakespeare once wrote: "All the world's a stage, And all the men and women merely players: They have their exits and their entrances; And one man in his time plays many parts." That said, here is Bill Krieger's tale of one man's memorable entrance—and exit—from the stage.

BILL KRIEGER

TAKE THE STAGE AND YOU'RE FINISHED!

he words appeared on the mirror of my dressing room six minutes before curtain time. I had just returned from a quick smoke break, and the huge red letters stared at me, dripping like paint. Or blood. This was my first performance in Las Vegas in eons, first performance anywhere in public, really, since—well, I can't even remember when. It was so long ago.

I stared at the ultimatum with disgust. Finished, am I? We'll just see about that.

I landed this spot at Augustus Palace and Casino on a sucker's bet. By rights, there was no way I should have won, but nonetheless I did.

I made the bet with one of the youngest managers I'd ever seen in a gambling house, and I'd been in them all. He held out his hand and introduced himself but I immediately forgot his name. That happens a lot when you reach a certain age.

He looked like a kid: flabby face, wispy mustache. But it was obvious to me he had a kind heart and didn't belong in the business. He took one glance at the liver spots on my hands and the suit I was wearing, left over from the Reagan Administration, and told me that I should skip the slots and save my money.

Magic Act

I'd been sitting in front of one of these new-fangled electronic one-armed bandits for the better part of two hours, bored, and mindlessly feeding in dollars as if they were dimes. Every few pulls I'd get a few coins back, but the tide receded as quickly as the coins in the complimentary red bucket they'd given me in case I hit the grand prize. On a whim, I asked him, "Are you interested in a side bet? That I can hit it big within the next three pulls?"

"Why don't you go home?" he said. "I think you've had too much to drink."

I smiled and said, "Sure have. The drinks are free."

"We have a great buffet, too," the kid manager said. "Why not put some food in your belly and come back another day?"

"Strange," I said. "A manager at the Augustus afraid I'll hit the jackpot despite the odds against me. They're like 650,000 to 1."

"What kind of bet?" he asked. I barely heard him over all the noise in the casino. There must have been a thousand people on the gambling floor: honeymooners, vacationers, widows and widowers, people in town for business cramming in a little R & R.

"I'm a magician with a stage act," I told him. "Here's the bet: if I hit, you let me work one of your smaller rooms. Haven't worked a place as nice as this in a hundred years."

The kid's wisps of mustache curled up in polite smile. "You do realize the quality of the magicians who perform at

Augustus? We're talking headliners the caliber of Penn and Teller."

"So you think I *can* hit the jackpot within the next three tries?"

The kid stared at me suspiciously. "Okay. What's your angle? You haven't been tampering with the machines, have you?"

I laughed. "You'd be a rich man if I did. Part of the deal is anything I win in the next three pulls belongs to you."

"And if you lose?"

I flashed him my most charming smile. Granted, it worked a lot better when I was in my twenties, but now, sixty-plus years later, not so much. You can only get by on charisma for so long.

"If I lose," I said, "I leave. And you get to feel good about yourself for putting people over profit, and saving an old man from gambling away his pension."

Frankly, I thought the kid didn't have any right being in the casino business in a town like Vegas. People lose their life savings here every day of the week, every week of the year. He was too soft for his job, but that suited my purposes fine. He smoothed down the wrinkles on his Armani suit and said, "You promise? Three tries and that's it."

"Oh, one more thing," I said. "If I lose, I leave. And you can feel good about saving an old man from gambling away his pension."

Magic Act

The kid looked at me with sad eyes. "*You do know you just said that, right?* Are you okay, old-timer? Are you here with a group? Is there anybody I can call for you?"

"Nope," I told him, "shook off my caretakers down at the Bellagio, and haven't felt this free in decades. They mean well, honest they do. But the folks down at the home don't give a fella time to breathe, if you know what I mean."

His smile was gentle and sad as he gestured to the machine. "Go ahead. Go for it."

"First chance," I announced. "Here goes nothing." I was playing one of the video poker slots and screamed, "Come on, Straight Flush!"

Up came the nine, ten, Jack and Queen of hearts…and a deuce of spades. I slipped in another dollar and the images of playing cards rolled again, coming up with a straight but not a flush. The machine spat out a few dollars, a tease to keep the suckers playing.

"Sorry, a little rusty here," I said. "But you know what they say: Third time's the charm."

The kid was as good as his word. Better, in fact.

When I hit a Royal Straight Flush on my third pull of the lever, he screamed right along with me, fully sharing my joy. Lights blinked, horns blared, and coins poured out of the mouth of my machine like silver vomit. My little container wasn't nearly big enough to catch all the falling loot. Red-suited assistants came to my rescue with more buckets than a fire brigade. It was mostly illusion, of course, and as a magician, I could appreciate that. The machine made enough of a fuss to attract maximum attention from the surrounding gamblers, but only a fraction of my haul actually spilled out right there. That was all for show. The manager now walked me over to the cashier where the real money would be handed to me in the form of a check.

I tried to hand my winnings over to the kid-manager but he wouldn't hear of it. "Beef up that retirement fund of yours, and try not to lose it. Too many people who win big just wind up giving it all back to us."

"But what about my performance? You said—"

"And I meant it. If you can pull off a magic trick half as good as winning that check, I'm happy to oblige. We have one of the top open mic venues in Vegas."

"Isn't that just karaoke?"

"Not at all. We host amazing amateur performances. From comedy club routines and solo guitarists to magic acts and fully orchestrated band jams. If you're itching to be the center of attention, there's no better place to be than the Augustus."

"Will I have a dressing room? Magicians need room to prepare."

"Sure."

I got off my stool and shook my head. "Not tonight, though. Tomorrow would be better."

"Not a problem."

Magic Act

"One last thing," I said. "Will I have a dressing room? Magicians need room to prepare."

⁂

The dressing room was small but luxurious. There wasn't really a lot that I had to prepare, just some standard tricks that I'd done back in the thirties, forties and fifties.

A part of me hoped that old expression would hold true: "Everything old will be new again." Acts today were all about the special effects, the lighting, rock and roll blaring in the background. I hoped that the old-fashioned elegance of white tie and cane that had gone out of style decades ago might suddenly seem fresh and new, given its long absence. The twenty-somethings in the audience probably never saw their like before.

Before I went on, I took a walk outside and bathed myself in all the artificial lights that ignited Vegas at night and made it breathtaking. It was a stroll through Wonderland. Waterfalls in front of the Bellagio lit up, then gushed and swayed in syncopation to the beautiful music the casino piped into the background.

Actually, the music in Vegas bothered me. Not the acts in the hotels; they were all top notch. But there were sound boxes on the street lamps throughout the strip, and on each corner, the speakers featured tunes sung by long dead singers like Sinatra, Martin and Sammy Davis Jr. I loved those guys.

Hearing them now, though, I felt like I was in a ghost town. I turned myself around and headed back to the Augustus. I needed time to dress for my act, and down enough complimentary drinks to calm my nerves. As I walked, I noticed my fingers tremble. This was not a good sign for a magician about to present himself as a master of sleight of hand and distraction. I grabbed a smoke and allowed it to quiet my nerves.

When I returned to my dressing room, I saw the crimson note that stained my mirror.

TAKE THE STAGE AND
YOU'RE FINISHED!

I thought I might know who'd written me the love note—but as soon as I remembered his name, it escaped me again. Jealousy motivates—and professional jealousy is even worse than the romantic kind. Still, I wondered why anyone—especially other magicians—would care a whit about me doing my old act one last time. Hell, if this *was* my finish, I intended to make it a BIG finish. And what better place to go out in style than to perform at Augustus Palace?

A bald head poked itself in my room and said, "You're on in ten, Gramps."

Magic Act

As soon as I heard him, I jumped up and stood in front of the mirror, my body trying to block the scarlet words from view. "I'm ready," I said.

"You sure you're up for this?" The kid manager was nowhere in sight. In his place was a strapping fellow in his mid-forties who introduced himself as the stagehand assigned to help me with my props. He threw me his name but I didn't catch it. Frankly, my hearing isn't what it used to be.

"I can talk you through some of the built-ins we have on the stage," he said, seeming oblivious to the words scrawled on the mirror. "Gimmicks and trap doors you can use in your act. Not a lot of time, though. But you might be able to use one." As he spoke, his brows wrinkled over eyes that studied me with a cross between dismay, skepticism and alarm. He pointed to the outfit I had laid out on the couch for myself.

"Is that what you're wearing, Gramps? Seems pretty old school. Got some costumes in the back might fit you. Wanna see 'em?"

"No, I'm fine," I said. "But, thank you. I intend to kick it… 'old school' …as you say."

He stood there shaking his head while I changed. I snugged on tuxedo pants with a satin line down their sides, slipped into a fluffy white shirt with ruffles beneath the collar and on the cuffs, then tugged on my black silk jacket. I spent a lot of time on my bow tie. A well-tied bow is the height of formal fashion, and it's become a lost art form, in my opinion. After my bow was perfect, I reached for my tuxedo's matching silk top hat, then grabbed a pair of white gloves from my pocket and slipped them on, spreading out my fingers wide at him.

The stagehand swiveled at the waist and pointed at the item behind him I'd rested against the wall. "What about that, Gramps? You're not really taking *that* out there with you?"

I reached behind him and snatched up the white-tipped black cane leaning there. "Can't be a magician without a cane," I said. "This whole look—white tie and tails, cane—is classic."

He looked at me as if I were the village idiot. "This ain't vaudeville, Gramps. You sure you want to go through with this? That's an audience of drinkers out there. They're gonna eat you alive, and wash you down with bourbon and beer chasers."

"I can handle the crowd," I said.

"How many showgirls you use in your act?"

"None," I said. "I like to grab a girl from the audience."

"A plant, huh?"

I gave him a knowing smile and he seemed to relax. Probably wouldn't have if he understood that I was doing this my way, not his, and whoever I chose was going to be the real deal, a civilian, not a plant.

"You know this whole look—white tie and tails, and cane—is classic," I said.

The stagehand shook his head and left me, closing the door behind him. He was muttering something but I couldn't tell what. Sounded like "stupid old fart" or some such but that may have been my imagination.

Frankly, my ears aren't as good as they used to be. When I watch TV shows and movies back at the Home, I use subtitles or miss a lot. I cleaned off the mirror with my handkerchief, another throwback to a more elegant time. The words in red wiped off without effort, as if they weren't there. A part of me was surprised that the stagehand never saw them. They were in full view at all times, but he never mentioned it, and I wondered why. Was he in cahoots with whoever wrote it?

The voice of the off-stage announcer boomed in the darkened room. It read out the line I'd handed him before stepping out onto the stage.

"Presenting… Doctor Alexander The Great, Master of the Mysterious Box of Blades."

As the stagehand predicted, I heard a collective groan from the audience as I walked out in my white tie and tails, top hat, and white gloves. In fairness to me, though, I was the fifth magic act in a revue billed as "A Magical Night In Vegas," and the only magician not adorned in sequins or wearing tight pants and a shirt open to the navel and flaunting abs of a movie star.

But to be welcomed to the stage with such rudeness was inexcusable. Worse, Penn and Teller—who I'd hoped to impress—could have been in the audience, but weren't. Guess they had no interest in amateur acts, and frankly, why should they? Silly of me to hope for it.

The stage lights blinded me as I stared out into the crowd, and the audience was little more than a sea of blackness. The room, smaller than I expected, probably sat about 200 people. Even in the dark, I knew many seats were unfilled.

"You've seen a lot of great acts so far," I began, "and I don't want to let you down. But don't prejudge me. I may be more than I seem."

That announcement led to a prolonged series of boos.

Fireworks flared up behind me. The stagehand or the manager was obviously trying to help me, though I'd requested no assistance. I ignored the negative reaction of the crowd and popped open a deck of ordinary playing cards that suddenly appeared in my white gloved hand as if by magic. I made the cards cascade from my left hand to my right, a shoulder's length apart. In the darkness, I saw dark head-shapes in the audience shaking with disapproval.

"Pick a card, any card," I dared the audience, as I fanned the cards out.

"Is this guy for real?" someone heckled.

"No, it's a comedy routine," came one loud response. "Give the old guy a chance."

Another voice screamed out, "Get off the stage, schmuck."

"Are you lost, old timer? Did you stray from the old folks' home?"

Additional comments came but I ignored them and waited for the audience to regain its composure. That was a mistake, though, because mockery rarely extinguishes itself. Rather, it feeds on itself and spreads.

The spotlight stayed on me, and I concentrated on the glow of its warmth. Such a long time since I'd been on a stage, and even though the crowd acted so poorly, I realized how much I missed the glamor of it all. If I could win over a crowd as tough as this one… perhaps, just perhaps … this didn't have to be my final bow. Win them over and scratch my way back into the limelight. Finished? Ha! This could be a new beginning for me.

I knew engaging the crowd would be tough. Today's magicians could seemingly make entire buildings disappear. Houdini himself might not be able to compete with them.

"Don't like card tricks?" I threw the cards up into the air and they disappeared just outside the circle of light in which I stood, as if defying gravity and refusing to return to ground. My spotlight blinked out and for a moment, I stood in darkness. I worried that the stagehand had taken matters into his own hands, and given me the hook. Instead, he was true to his word and I heard the rattle of my props moving into place behind me.

The stage lights burst on and revealed a long, coffin-like box. An old-fashioned dressing screen stood across the stage from it, its three folding panels bent slightly allowing it to stand. Back in the day, countless homes featured these screens so women could change their clothes while maintaining their sense of dignity and privacy.

"What you are about to see will amaze you." I swept a shaking hand first toward the dressing screen, then to the coffin on the other side of the stage. "I present to you for your entertainment … The Mysterious Box of Blades."

"The geezer's gonna saw a girl in half. That gag's older than he is."

A fresh round of boos hurled up at me from the audience.

"But first," I shouted over them, "I need a volunteer."

My casino friend must have been watching my act and decided to help. At first, I thought he was going to pull the plug on me and escort me from the stage. Then, I saw that benign, pudgy face of his, and stopped worrying. I guessed incorrectly that he was interrupting my act in order to warn the audience to quiet down or be removed from the theater "We don't treat any performer this way at Augustus," I expected him to say.

He was a good man but confrontation wasn't his way, though. Not even with an unruly crowd. Reminded me a bit of the son I never had and never wanted. Why he was allowing me this chance I'll never know. However, he was as good as his word, and surprised me with what he did next.

Instead of bringing threats, he brought treats: eye candy to be exact.

He waved into the wings and strutted out with one of the tallest, most beautiful showgirls I'd ever seen. She was a long-legged redhead wearing fishnet stockings and high heels, and a fancy black bikini outfit with leather straps that wrapped around her belly. Her short sequined jacket featured see-through sleeves that reached down to her wrists. A pink boa wrapped around her left elbow and dangled to her knees. On her head, she wore an elaborate headpiece with feathers that complemented the color of the boa. She towered over my benefactor, the manager, who delivered his straight line as he joined me on the stage: "Did I hear someone say they needed a volunteer?"

The crowd roared with catcalls and laughter, clearly excited by this new turn of events.

I knew what they were thinking. That I sang the beginning of my act in falsetto, a set up for the tune I was really about to sing. Perhaps some even thought that I was a young man masquerading as old. There was a movie like that called "Bad Grampa" or some such, where that was the running gag. Don't know how it did at the box office. Never saw it myself. I hate the way older people are portrayed in the movies and on TV. The moment I see someone of age portrayed as a dunderheaded fool, I pick myself up and leave.

"No, no, no," I screamed into the audience. "That will never do."

My new friend from the casino gave me a hard look and I smiled at him in return.

"No, what I need is a lady from the audience," I screamed over the crowd. "Someone exactly like…" I pointed a shaky finger and used it to trace a path through the audience. It was still so dark in the theater that I couldn't see what anyone looked like. However, my finger lingered momentary on four attractive shapes in the front row, two of which were painfully thin. Then it settled on a fifth figure, further back, which abruptly turned its head to look away.

"Yes," I said. "Someone exactly like you. Please come up to the stage."

The woman in the audience appeared to have come with a bevy of friends. I could hear them laughing and giggling, urging their friend to join me.

It took a moment or two, before she reluctantly complied and made her way up to me.

As she took the stage and entered its light, the catcalls ended. A new round of taunts, hisses and jeers replaced them. The woman I'd chosen was neither tall nor short, neither beautiful nor homely. She was somewhat heavy set, and the crowd booed her.

Though my face never showed it, I sneered at them … this crowd filled with out of shape middle-age men, their beer bellies dangling over their belt buckles… all judging a woman solely on her dress size. The hypocrisy of the moment sickened me.

Yet the trick about to begin was of my own invention, and depended on my volunteer carrying some extra pounds. I really couldn't blame the audience for their reaction, as I was counting on it. That made me as guilty and as judgmental as the lot of them, I suppose.

"What's your name, darling?" I asked her.

"Rachel," she murmured.

"Thank you for volunteering, Rachel. I think you may enjoy this."

Rachel stared down at her flats. She was wearing black business slacks that fit her well and a matching top. My volunteer looked uncomfortable as I stared at her.

"Just one question before we begin," I said. "What's your name, darling?"

She stared up at me with confused blue eyes. "Rachel," she said.

"Well, Rachel. Behind this dressing screen—" I pointed at it—"you will find a very special outfit. If you would be so kind: Please change into it."

Rachel looked at me as if I were crazy then gazed out into the audience, looking for her friends. I knew she couldn't see them. Until the show is over and the house lights come back up, the audience is always kept in the dark. Rachel gamely nodded agreement and made her way to the dressing screen as if heading to the gallows. She disappeared behind it.

A backlight burst into life behind the thin material of the screen, creating a silhouette of the plucky young woman as she changed her clothes. As the audience watched, the black shadow removed its top and struggled out of pants. The crowd began laughing at her.

The laughter stopped just a few moments later. It ended as soon as Rachel struggled into the special fishnet stockings that I'd left for her on a chair. The outline of her thick legs transformed as she pulled on her new tights. The silhouette of her waist shrunk, as well, as her shadow pulled up the pantyhose.

"Oh. My. God!" Rachel shrieked from behind the curtain. "This is …NOT… possible."

The crowd grew silent.

The hands of the dark shadow behind the curtain held up another garment and pulled it over her head, and her arms slipped into sleeves. As Rachel tugged at the waist of her new jacket, her arms and waistline transfigured now, too. Backlit, it appeared that there was another person altogether behind the dressing screen. This new silhouette then snugged itself into a bikini bottom and adjusted its straps.

I had the audience's attention now. "Thinning Black is what I called this trick," I announced. "And now, I proudly present to you …"

Magic Act

I forgot the girl's name again and someone from the audience screamed it to me: "Rachel, you moron."

I could feel the mood of the audience change. Grow impatient with me again.

"Yes, of course. And now, I present—ta, da—Rachel."

The screen rose up into the rafters on ropes, revealing a woman who looked nothing like the girl who had disappeared behind the screen. Instead, stood a slender woman who wore the exact outfit of the showgirl the crowd had seen earlier. Slimmer, Rachel was a knockout.

From the audience came a small applause, one that I call "pity applause." This surprised me, as I was expecting whistles and catcalls. Instead, the same few voices that had been loud earlier assaulted me again.

"Lame," cried one.

"Fraud," screamed another.

"You just switched girls behind the screen," yelled a third. "What kind of *doofus* trick is that?"

"No, that's Rachel," I swore. "Really, it is."

As the stagehand lowered the dressing screen back into place on the stage, I tapped the breast pocket of my tux with my cane three times, and said, "Maybe her outfit needs one final touch." Then I pulled out a sequined hat with pink and purple feathers just like the showgirl had modelled. Admittedly, this part of the trick was a little cheesy, like pulling an unending handkerchief from beneath the cuff of your sleeve. It was meant to inject a little bit of humor during the audience's stunned silence.

But the silence that greeted me was not one of awe. My fumbling the girl's name had broken the spell, the immediacy of the moment. Instead, the silence was short lived and quickly morphed into a new round of increasingly louder boos.

My casino friend shrugged his shoulders and, escorted by the showgirl on his arm, disappeared into the wings. I figured the hook was coming soon, so I had to get my act into gear before I really was returned to my nursing home.

"I appreciate your enthusiastic response," I told the crowd. "As the late great Jackie Gleason—star of the classic TV show, *The Honeymooners*, once said—and I apologize if I misquote this—but, 'anyone can laugh or applaud at an act. It's the natural thing to do. But it takes real effort to heckle and boo someone on stage,'" I mimed downing a drink from a shot glass. "So spare me the applause," I crooned. "Because it's really *the booze* I love."

Not a chuckle. Not a giggle. Not even the sound of an exasperated sigh.

I almost said to the audience, "I know you're out there. I can hear you breathing," but resisted the overwhelming urge.

Instead, I used my most menacing voice and hissed a warning at the crowd.

"What you are about to see now has only been performed once before on any stage, and resulted in a young woman's death. If you are weak at heart—if the sight of blood causes you to scream—if you believe that seeing this fine young woman brutally dismembered will scar you for life, I WARN you. Leave the theatre now."

Five people from the audience got up and left, muttering to themselves. When they were gone, I raised my hands and said, "The rest of you have been warned. You can no longer leave. I now lock the theater doors … magically."

The theater's surround sound system kicked in and the click of locks danced from one exit to another. The crowd grew silent again, their expectations seemingly on the rise.

I took my volunteer by the hand and walked her over to the coffin standing on the far side of the stage. "Just one question before we begin," I said to her. "What's your name, darling?"

"RACHEL!" the crowd screamed at me.

A prop man raced out from the wings with a handsaw and pressed it into my hands.

"Oh, crap," screamed a now-familiar voice from the crowd. "I knew it. He's going to saw a girl in half. Shoulda left when we had the chance."

That line got the biggest laugh of the night.

I whispered to Rachel not to worry, that what I said to the crowd was nothing more than dramatic flair. "Do you trust me?"

Rachel's mouth curved into a spirited grin. "Are you kidding me? I would trust anyone who gave me free liposuction." At her response, the audience gave her a generous round of laughter and applause.

I brought out a small stepladder from behind the dressing screen where Rachel had changed outfits earlier, carried it over to the coffin, and held her hand as she climbed up and slipped into the box. The box spun around on its wheels under my guidance, and with each turn, I knocked on the wooden panels that encased her with my cane.

"Good," I said. "But this?" I flexed the handsaw that the stagehand had given me. "This seems too flimsy to cut through such a thick wooden box." My fingers curled around the tool's handle and tossed it into the wings. "This won't cut through anything that isn't already cut. This hacksaw is the fraud, my friends. Not I. Not Doctor Alexander The Great, Master of the Mysterious Box of Blades."

I disappeared again behind the dressing curtain, and emerged from it holding a chain saw. As I pulled at its starter chain, its roar thundered in the darkened theater. "Now this," I said, "*this* can cut through ANYTHING."

From the corner of my eye, I saw my casino friend mouth the words, "What are you doing?" I pretended not to see him and strutted across the stage. My step was so light it felt like I was dancing to the hum of the weapon vibrating in my hand.

Magic Act

To the crowd, I roared, "The Texas Chainsaw Massacre has nothing on ME!"

I raised the blade and headed toward the on-stage coffin. When it sliced into the wooden box it sent splinters flying through the air, and Rachel screamed. Blood gushed onto the stage as if a volcano had erupted. People in the audience screamed. Many ran to the exits at the back of the theater as fast as they could. They found every door locked.

"Return to your seats!" My voice thundered its command. With no exits open to them, they complied like mindless drones. "You now bear witness to the greatest magic act of all time, taught to me by the ancient wizards of Xanadu, who first performed it for Kublai Khan in his summer palace ages ago. Anyone can saw a woman in half. But have you ever seen a woman sliced into quarters? Sliced and diced into eighths?"

I revved up my chainsaw as if it were a racing car, filling the theater with noise. Was it just my imagination or could I hear teeth rattling in the audience? I smiled and sliced the top of Rachel into two, and then again, cutting her once at the throat and leaving only her head. Blood poured from her gaping wounds, a gusher of death.

No one moved from their seats.

My friend in the wings pulled out his cell phone, and I heard him call for security. Within moments, four armed men unlocked the doors at the back of the theater and raced down the aisles, guns drawn. They screamed for me to stop, but I was prepared. The moment they came within three feet of me, a huge hunter's net appeared from a hidden compartment beneath the stage and swallowed them up, jerking them into the air. Their guns clattered to the floor as they dropped.

"No one interrupts a magic act. It's considered rude, and it spoils the grand finale."

I turned back to Rachel and asked her if she was still alive.

Her eyes blinked back at me. "Yes."

The audience gave up an audible sigh of relief.

My chainsaw revved up again, and continued its deadly business. I dissected the bottom portion of the coffin now, halving this half as I had the earlier one. Then I split each quarter in half yet again. The amount of blood that stained the stage floor was horrific. "Are you still all right in there, Rachel?" I asked.

"Yes, I'm fine."

The audience gasped.

"You," I called out to the man who had been heckling me the loudest. "Come to me. Be careful, though. The floor here is slippery with blood."

My eyes latched onto his and became hypnotic. The fearful expression on his face left me with a great joy. He had no idea why he was complying with my request. It was as if he had no will of his own.

"Just one question before we begin," I said. "What's your name, sir?"

"M-Marty," he stammered.

"Marty, have you ever played Three-Card Monty?"

"Y-Yes."

"There are eight pieces of this woman on stage right now. What I want you to do is shuffle them around. Are you all right with that Marty?"

"Y-Yes."

"Good. Just one question before we begin. Please tell the audience your name."

Each section of Rachel's coffin was on wheels and slid easily from one side of the stage to another under Marty's quivering fingers. When he was finished, Marty said, "Can I leave now? I want to leave now."

"No." I laughed. "You above all, my disbelieving friend, need to see this trick close up. I want you to leave wondering how I did it. I want you not to believe your own eyes."

Marty did his job well. While I covered my eyes with my top hat, Marty slid around the many pieces of Rachel. When he said he was finished, I slowly lowered my hat, then flicked it upwards and allowed it land—perfectly—in place upon my head.

With my vision no longer obscured, I confess that the trick seemed a tad more difficult than I remembered it. With the all the pieces laid out in front of me, I suddenly felt stumped. Wasn't quite sure which piece went where. Wasn't clear how my big finish would end.

The head of course was easy. It was poking out of the box, so I knew that went on top.

The feet, exposed, were also easy to place, as were the segments of Rachel's legs.

But after I settled six of her pieces into place, I froze. Two pieces of her upper body remained and seemed to fit together regardless of how I placed them, Of course, only one way could be right… and, unfortunately, all decisions were final. Once I put the segments back together and tapped them three times with my white-tipped cane, the assembly of Rachel would be complete… and more than complete. It would also be irreversible.

I tugged at my pursed lips. Where had I made my mistake? I think it may have been in making my box slices too even. Variations were the key to the trick. Varying the sizes of the wooden coffin slivers, ever so slightly, was the blueprint for reassembling them. For all intents and purposes, this part of the trick wasn't different from shaving down playing cards in order to be able to "read" them. How had I forgotten such an important element of my most mysterious trick?

My mind reached back to the time I performed in Vegas at Caesar's—

"FREEZE!"

Two men in white jackets suddenly appeared at the back of the theater. The house lights blinked on, and I looked out over my audience. Saw that they'd become like statues, frozen in place, their positions awkward and candid, trapped in the moment. The two men followed the same route down the theater's aisles that security had earlier, and I recognized them both. Because I can never remember names, I call the taller of the two Abbott and the shorter one Costello. I had loved Abbott and Costello when radio was as popular as TV is today, and families gathered around the big brown box to listen to their famous vaudeville routines. "Who's on First?" was my all-time favorite.

When they reached the stage, I saw the familiar logo on the breast pocket of their jackets:

Wizards Assisted Living and
Retirement Home of Miami

"Doc," said Abbott. "You can't go disappearing on us like this."

"We left you a message," Costello piped in. "Take the stage, do your act, and when you finish, you're *finished—no more outings without permission or supervision.* So hurry up, and put her back together. Let's get you back to the home."

"I can't," I said. "I forgot how the end goes. If I get it wrong I could kill her."

Abbott studied the pieces already in place and nodded his approval. "Six out of eight pieces, Doc. Not bad for a mage your age. You still got the magic touch."

"I hate myself for not knowing this," I said. "The last part is on the tip of my tongue."

"Doc, would you like some help?"

I nodded, and Abbot whispered something to the box. All the blood on the stage seeped into the floor and faded away. Then he switched the last two pieces around, and told me it was good to go.

"Do I still get to tap it?"

Costello said, "We're finished, Doc."

"Do I still get to tap it?"

Abbott smiled at me. "Sure, Doc. You can tap it."

My fingers curled tighter around my white tipped cane and tapped on the reassembled box three times. The box melded back into one.

I opened up its lid and Rachel sat up.

"Good as new," I said. "And I thank you for being a good sport, and such a big part of my show."

Costello frowned. "Did she look like that when you started all this craziness?"

I stared down at my feet. "Yes," I said.

"Put her back, Doc. Or I will."

"But she's been such a great sport."

Costello folded his arms across his chest. "Magic has no place in today's world, Doc. You shouldn't have left the home."

"I was just taking a walk. I think I lost my way."

Abbott chuckled. "This is Vegas, Doc. The Home's in Miami. I think you need to be more careful with your travel spells."

"I miss Las Vegas."

Abbott turned to Rachel. "Ma'am, is this how you looked when Doc started the trick?"

Rachel was now a lean, long-legged beauty more stunning than any showgirl. She reminded me of my late wife.

"Leave her alone," I said, moving in front of her.

Abbott sighed. To me, he said, "Did you even ask her if this is what she wanted?" He turned to Rachel. "Ma'am, do you want me to change you back? This look is not unique. He's done this at least four times before. Or would you prefer to—"

Rachel's face dazzled with her grin. "Oh, God, yes! Please. Keep me this way!"

Costello unfolded his arms. "Doc, if we let you keep the girl the way she is, you promise not to disappear on us like this again?"

"Of course," I said.

"Ok, then. Then let's make with the magic and go."

"A deal," I said. "Rachel, it was a pleasure meeting you. Please. Enjoy your life. The moments pass too quickly, and memories can disappear like magic."

I took the hands of the men sent to retrieve me and we made a small circle. "Just one question before we go," I said, my head spinning back to look at her one last time. "What's your name, darling?"

The Book of the Shadow of the Moon

Everything that we see is a shadow cast by that which we do not see.

- Martin Luther King, Jr.

To contemplate is to look at shadows.

- Victor Hugo

SIX

THE FIRST CENSOR'S STATEMENT

DONNA ROYSTON

Donna Royston edits papers for an actuarial science journal and finds relief from advanced probability distributions by writing speculative fiction. Here, we are introduced to a group of learned scholars devoting a day to the practice of poetry. Strange and wonderful images abound, both natural and manmade. But a word of caution: Donna's characters are sometimes not quite what they seem. Careful readers are in for a treat. You have been warned.

Donna Royston

Given to T'au Hsun of the Emperor's Guard, personal emissary of the Son of Heaven

n the tenth year of the Reign of Everlasting Harmony, on the third day of the third moon (which, of course, was today), we met here at the country home of our friend Wang Hsi-chih the calligrapher. He had invited us once again to celebrate the Water Festival at the Orchid Pavilion, where we would wash away the evil spirits of winter and drink and compose poetry.

And so I arrived here with my servants while the day was young and the sun was just beginning to sift through the cherry blossoms. In that ethereal light, with the warm breeze making its quiet song in the bamboo leaves, winter seemed a thousand years away.

"My esteemed friend," Wang Hsi-chih bowed in welcome, smiling widely, as I stepped from my sedan chair, "it is a glorious day for poetry, is it not?"

"Heaven smiles on our gathering," I replied. "May we reach the level of inspiration—and drunkenness—that we were so fortunate to attain last year."

The First Censor's Statement

"And here approaches our last guest, himself almost a portrait of spring," said Wang Hsi-chih. I turned to look.

It would have been impossible not to admire Lu Tiao as he rode up on his white horse. He smiled at us and leaped from the horse's back, coming to a graceful and light landing—who would not want to be young again and in such high spirits, attired in gleaming silk of the finest work, embroidered blue, gold, and black, dark hair gleaming against pale yellow tunic? He could have been the Immortal youth Lan Ts'ai-ho himself, so beautiful that the gods dispatched a celestial stork to seize him and carry him up to heaven. His face was radiant as he greeted us. "Master Wang—I have had a glorious ride this morning from Shao-hsing. I thought I would be late, but I see I have arrived in time."

"Just in time," Wang Hsi-chih said. "Everyone is now present."

To tell you a little about us: we are all, except for Wang Hsi-chih, government bureaucrats who serve the emperor's court in some way. Perhaps one might live on one's poetry if one lived as the birds, without the need for paying for food, lodging, or clothes. As we are not birds, however, we are functionaries for our living and poets for our pleasure. Meng Wei is Scribe of Edicts and Laws, Han Tzu is Historian in Charge of Archives, Hsiao Kan is Collator of Texts, Kao Fu is Instructor of Classics at the Imperial University, Tu Shen is

Adjutant-Under-the-Right-Commandant-Under-the-Crown-Prince, and I, Sun Ch'o, am First Censor of Lu-shan.

But we knew that Lu Tiao of the radiant face was different from the rest of us in an important respect: while we were destined to live our lives in official obscurity, it was said (as you probably are aware) that he had the attention of the emperor and would soon be receiving a token of the emperor's favor in the form of an important post, the first stepping stone to great power and an illustrious career. His youthful circuit of banquets, riding, hunting, swordplay, cockfights, dancing, parties, and poetry improvisations would give way to work and politics all too soon. In a few years, we knew, he would be too important to come to gatherings of humble men such as us.

Wang Hsi-chih led us to his gardens, where the men of our poetry group and other guests awaited, admiring the beauty of the landscape. Tu Shen was talking quietly to Kao Fu and Meng Wei. He looked very somber, as though a sadness weighed on his spirits. I saw him fix his eyes on Lu Tiao with unusual intensity, but Lu Tiao did not seem to notice. Tu Shen is by his nature rather melancholy at times, without any particular cause, but in this case I easily surmised the reason for his mood. He has a conservative taste in clothes, and he was probably offended by the daring of Lu Tiao's garb. At the same time he was too courteous to give a sign—therefore he modified his expression to a general appearance of gloom.

"What news from the Imperial City?" I asked Meng Wei.

"Nothing to speak of," he replied.

"That is indeed newsworthy," I said, humorously, "that there is nothing to report."

"Gentlemen, make yourselves comfortable," said Wang Hsi-chih. "I think everyone knows the rules? Where a cup stops, that person must give us a poem related to spring, or else pay the penalty and drink the cup. Of course, if you give us a poem and still want to drink the cup, you may do so."

I chose a delightful spot where the stream made a little curve around a soft mossy bank. To my left grew a small clump of willow, only a few feet high, starting to feather out with tender new leaves, and I sat down with the trunk of a blossoming peach tree at my back. Petals fluttered down around me. I spread my roll of paper before me, ink pot to my right and brush in my hand, in readiness, and then I leaned back against the tree and looked up into its branches and the sky beyond. It was a lovely view with the petals falling—as I watched, a swallow, quickly followed by another, darted through the flower-snow and was gone.

Meng Wei sat down on the opposite side of the stream, removed his shoes, and dabbled his bare feet in the stream, smiling in pleasure.

I began composing. After some thought, and a bit of nibbling on the end of my brush, I had my first poem of the day. I inscribed the characters with some flourish. Then I looked up from my paper.

Lu Tiao was writing furiously, so he had a poem in progress; Meng Wei was gazing abstractedly into the stream.

A lotus leaf with a small cup of wine on it came floating peacefully down the stream, meandered a bit in an eddy where the stream curved, and then continued on its way. I was happy to let it go. I only had one poem so far, and it was early to start drinking. There would be more cups floating down the current in a short while.

I mused, searching for new inspiration.

My thoughts wandered, what with the pleasantness of the sunshine and the gentle touch of the breeze. I had been home for the past ten days with an illness, a remnant of one of winter's evil spirits, and this was my first day away from home during that time. I stretched my back and scratched my ankle. Ah… I considered whether I should follow Meng Wei's example and bathe my feet in the stream.

Another lotus leaf with its wine-cup passenger came voyaging down the stream. It caught on a rock just in front of me.

I saw Meng Wei smile. "You have been selected," he said.

I stood up, and those who were near enough to hear me all turned their attention my way.

"A poem in honor of this glorious day," I said, as introduction.

The First Censor's Statement

New peach blossoms have opened
Soft in the early light.
Yesterday's petals drift down
Swirled by swallows' flight.
The willow is sprinkled
With petals pink and white.

"Well done," said Tu Shen.

"Elegantly crafted," said Kao Fu.

Lu Tiao smiled, but said nothing.

We went back to our composing (or, as the case might be, relaxing. Last year the final tally was: eleven of us wrote two poems, fifteen wrote one poem, and sixteen didn't write any. You may conclude that some of Wang Hsi-chih's friends are less serious than others about poetry, and those who only wish to admire nature and talk and drink wine are just as welcome as the poets).

And so the time passed pleasantly. Several cups passed by without being caught. Far upstream, someone was reciting a poem, but I could not hear it and did not care to walk up there. Another cup came rollicking down the stream and caught on a bit of gravel in front of young Lu Tiao.

He stood and waited for our attention. Then he said, "The beauty of nature is all very well, but there needs to be a beautiful lady to ornament it—"

The nightingale's ecstasy
spills from the bamboo grove
Thrilling the night air. Greater joy
Seizes me: a girl walks under the full moon,
Trailing her silk robe in the dew.

His voice swelled as he recited, and a faint warmth suffused his face. *This is a boy in love*, I thought, pleased at my perceptiveness.

We lauded his verse for its beautiful imagery and passion. Scarcely had we finished when another lotus leaf floated down the stream and eddied near Tu Shen. He stood up and there was a long pause; he was composing as we waited. In the silence I could hear the pleasant cry of the cuckoo in the grove—the very sound of spring. Then Tu Shen recited:

His beautiful hen
Is left alone
While the nightingale attends
His lord moon;
The cuckoo consoles her.

The First Censor's Statement

A very clever conceit, I thought. And very neat, tying the nightingale from Lu Tiao's poem to the cuckoo that sang so near us.

To answer your question—does it mean anything?—well, it is a traditional ironic theme: I can think of a dozen poems very similar to it without straining my memory. But perhaps you think it odd that the setting of the poem was at night—here is the beauty of a spring morning and you would expect shining, light-filled ideas to be the stuff we would be working with? Sometimes, you must understand, the poetic imagination is retrograde: it imagines what is not there; it behaves illogically. Contentment makes it contemplate terror, and hardship makes it dream of peace. Why else the practice of celebrating spring by lamenting how quickly it passes? This backwardness is shown again in Lu Tiao's next work. He jumped up and took the next cup without waiting for it to stop of its own accord—his poems had outpaced the cups and he was impatient—and he said:

The full moon blazes
Overhead, and I cannot sleep.
The night is endless.
Far away I hear her voice –
I run outside to answer.

His eyes were intense as he looked at Tu Shen. Then he sat down again, haughtily, I thought. He meant his poem as a reproach to Tu Shen's cynical work, that was plain. Of course, the young will always be talking of, dreaming about, pure love: they think it is the only subject. And those to whom art comes easily, in a flood of inspiration, always disdain the craftsman and the ironic voice. Irony, I think—do you agree?—is the quality that one appreciates more and more in art as one matures. I find that I can scarcely write a direct outpouring of sentiment anymore. I am always seeking the short, the understated, that which says what it does not say. I do not mean that I cannot appreciate Lu Tiao's work: I think it is very good and at times I have been envious. I will recite some of his best poems that he has created in the past, if you wish. No? Then I will continue.

Five cups passed all of us by, going on to those downstream, out of our hearing. (But we do have the texts of all the poems that were made, if you wish to read the ones I did not hear, or if you want to check my memory regarding the ones I did hear; Wang Hsi-chih recorded all of the poems on a scroll at the end of the day, just as he did last year. Ask him: he will show you the scroll.)

Wang Hsi-chih's servants were very busy, bustling back and forth, some of them catching the cups that made it past everyone, others taking cups back upstream, still others collecting the cups that had been stopped and the ones that had been drunk. And some filled the cups and set them afloat, of course, and others brought us food, so we lacked for nothing to be comfortable. And I sat and took my ease and watched the swallows, the bamboo waving in the breeze, the flowing water.

Tu Shen received the next cup. He said:

The frozen heart of a great river
Does not grow softer in the spring
When he becomes a raging torrent.

This poem, of course, was suggested by the landscaping all around us, which, as I mentioned, is very fine: the stream represents a river, rocks are set into the ground to represent mountains. The thawing of the river signifies spring. This poem was also well praised.

The next to receive a cup was Kao Fu. He recited:

The dragon holds a pearl in his mouth.
But when it loses its luster
He crushes it.

A dragon may symbolize the emperor, sometimes, that is true. But there is nothing puzzling here for one who holds the key. Are you not a lover of gardening? Ah, if you were, you would recognize Dragon-with-a-Pearl-in-his-Mouth as a type of peony, highly coveted. It is a brilliant red with a small cluster of white petals in the center. Wang Hsi-chih has a very beautiful specimen in his garden.

Since you continue to question me about what these poems mean, I will elaborate on some general principles, as I understand them. It is a common misconception among those who do not cultivate the art to believe that in a poem, things always mean something else. They do not think that there is anything worth saying about a caterpillar, a bird, or a moonlit night. They are blind to the art of words. A well-chosen phrase or perfect image is the same to them as the most ill-chosen and inapt—indeed, the unskilled may find the poorer work preferable, if they recognize a familiar sentiment. Please do not take offense. But think how it would pain you if I or another one, unable to differentiate between good and bad, praised an incompetent swordsman or condemned a skillful rider. You understand? Consider the sword hilt upon which your hand rests. It is solid to the touch, made of bronze, inscribed with a design of clouds and inlaid with gold and silver; the handle is of fine wood, the grip covered with ray skin. You know that it is indeed a sword, is that not true? Your hand, your eyes do not allow any doubt. Consider further what you would think of someone who told you that a sword was actually a tongue, or a man. You would think that person lacked fundamental understanding of the world.

Thus I explain that a poem means what it says. A poet labors to make you truly and vividly see what he describes. A symbol is not a thing that hides another thing. It is itself, in plain view. It exists to be noticed and contemplated, but not to change what is.

I am sorry to confuse you.

Meng Wei then, at last, had a turn. He stood and we waited to hear while he prepared himself. He spoke very feelingly, for he is always affected by his poems.

A shining plum blossom
Lived for a day.
The dew lay on her like pearls.
She will never know autumn.

It was astonishing—and very affecting—to see and hear his emotion. It was so powerful that we received this poem in silence and considered it.

And then Lu Tiao of the radiant face stood, and I could see that the poem had also affected him. He stared at Meng Wei, who only looked back at him without speaking, and then he looked at each of us, in turn, his gaze never resting. He did not even notice that he had upset his ink pot and a black stain was coiling down the stream.

Now do you understand what it is like to be a poet? We find tragedy in the passing of a delicate flower, for although the flower is only a flower, it reminds us of things in our lives that are fragile and loved and fleeting.

Wang Hsi-chih walked up to Lu Tiao—I had not even been aware that he had approached—and he took him in an embrace and released him and said:

"You are in the grip of intense feeling, Lu Tiao. You should express it in a poem so that you do not lose it."

But Lu Tiao could not speak. He struggled, but the creative spirit had fled, and no words came. He was staring into space, almost as though dazed, when our eyes were attracted by another cup floating slowly down the stream. It stopped beside us. Wang Hsi-chih bent down and picked it up. He said:

The lowly herb bends
And will not with the winds contend;
In yielding it is preserved,
The storm is merely dew.

After this, Kao Fu took the cup from him and spoke:

Range after range of mountains
Recede into clouds and haze:
Mist wets the pilgrim's hat brim,
Dew soaks his hem.
With sandals on his feet
And staff in his hand
He looks behind at the dusty world
As a land of dreams.

Then he gave the cup to Lu Tiao, who drank it. He stood in silence with the cup in his hands and I could see he was composing. We all waited. At last he handed me the empty cup and said:

The golden prince, lord of the sky
Courses his burning steeds across heaven.
Across the eight corners of the land
The boar and hare bow in homage
The lordly stag bends his head
The flying partridge prostrates himself
Before the keeper of life.

What can the sun show me
That I will desire?

The night is deep and endless
Far away I hear her voice
And I run to answer.

And then he left the garden, walking back toward the house and the road. When we finished, in the afternoon, he was gone.

And so, you see, while I understand that you are angry to have arrived too late, it cannot be helped: Lu Tiao is gone. He did not leave word with anyone to say why he left early or where he was going. I hope I have not been overlong in answering your questions. I judge by your expression that you find us very foolish, grown men with our heads in the clouds.

I am saddened to hear of Lady Shan's death. It seems only yesterday that she was a child—Little Plum Blossom, her father called her. Neither I, nor anyone else here, knew that Lu Tiao had offended Lord Shan. We spent the day making poems—merely that—as is fitting for loyal subjects of the Son of Heaven who gather to celebrate the Water Festival. The final tally was this: one of us wrote three poems, nine wrote two poems, sixteen wrote one poem, and eleven didn't write any.

SEVEN

EMISSARY: TUITION MONEY

LIZ HAYES

Liz Hayes is an analyst at a think tank inside the Beltway. She writes *Lord of the Rings* fan fiction under the penname *Uvatha the Horseman.* Liz is most intrigued by Khamûl, second-in-command of the Nazgûl, sometimes called The Shadow of the East.

In her novel *Emissary*, Liz seeks to explain why Urzahil accepts a position offered by the Dark Lord. The following piece in an excerpt from that novel.

Urzahil of Umbar, the baseborn son of a great lord, was raised in a noble household among his father's legitimate sons. Of all the children, Urzahil most resembled his father in looks and interests and was the favorite, much to the dismay of his father's lady wife. Then his father died unexpectedly, and Urzahil found himself suddenly homeless, with the same aspirations he'd always had but no way in the world to achieve them.

hen at last Urzahil reached the tavern and livery stable that was both his place of employment and, unknown to the innkeeper, his residence, he crossed the courtyard and went straight to the stables to see to the horses.

He found a shovel and lifted a pile of manure into the wheelbarrow, then muscled the heavy barrow outside and dumped its contents onto the dung heap.

In his mind, he was at court, his silk robes sweeping the floor, the chain of office heavy around his neck. One nobleman and then another sought him out, asking a favor, spreading rumor, seeing alliance. Urzahil was in his element.

He could read the ebb and flow of court intrigue with the skill of a sea captain studying ocean currents.

I always thought this is what I'd be doing when I came of age. I just assumed it would be metaphorical.

It took longer than usual to muck out the stalls since he hadn't done it in the morning, and it was now late afternoon. When he finished, he carried bucket after bucket of water, then gave each of the horses an extra measure of oats, to make up for neglecting them this morning.

A big auburn stallion rubbed its broad forehead against his chest, either affectionate or itchy, it was hard to tell with horses. Normally that was something Urzahil liked, but today he wasn't in the mood.

"Oh, right. I feed you, I water you, I shovel your poop. You should be grateful."

Urzahil had stayed up late studying the night before, and his eyes were closing. When he was finished with the horses, he picked up his satchel and climbed the ladder to the hayloft for a few hours' sleep before he began his shift in the tavern. The heavy satchel bumped against his hip with each rung, and the noise woke the pigeons in the rafters, who stirred with a soft cooing and flapping of wings.

His head cleared the platform, and he froze. The hay was thinner near the edge of the loft, and piled up higher further back.

What if someone had seen his belongings, and realized he was living here? Or worse, found the purse with his tuition money in it? He sprinted across the loft and clawed through the hay in the corner where the ceiling was low. There were his clothes, and the school essays he had been saving. He kept digging. His fingers brushed the leather bag, fat with coins. He scooped it up and held it against his chest until his pulse returned to normal.

Urzahil emptied the leather pouch into his hand and counted the money. Tuition for the second term was due in three days. He didn't have quite enough, but he was only short by a little; two days' worth of tips on a good night, or five days on an average night.

What would bring someone up here? An amorous encounter? Ick. More likely, they just needed some hay. This was the hayloft, after all. He had no reason to think that anyone who worked in the stables was a thief, but he no longer felt comfortable leaving his money in the loft, unguarded.

What to do? He could hide it inside the feed bin, but he wasn't the only one who took grain from it to feed the horses. Sometimes a traveler low on funds would carry water and shovel manure in exchange for bed and board.

Emissary: Tuition Money

Urzahil hung his purse on his belt, but it had gotten so fat and round, it would show through the fabric. He put it in his coat pocket instead. He would hide his coat under the bar near the cash box where it would be safe.

))) ● ● ● ● ● ● ● (((

Urzahil crossed the inn yard and pushed open the door under the Sign of the Boiling Frog, jingling the door chimes as he came in.

The innkeeper stood behind the bar, rinsing tankards. "Yule's almost here, we're going to be busy tonight. Set up some extra trestle tables in the middle of the room."

Urzahil nodded, and hung his coat on the peg near the door. He put on his apron, brought the trestle tables up from the root cellar and set them up in the middle of the common room, then brought up the long benches that went with them. He carried a keg up from the cellar, and set out extra tankards.

The dinner rush began in earnest. Urzahil took drink orders, carried heavy trays, and fetched extra loaves of bread. He set twelve tankards in front of twelve customers seated the length of one of the trestle tables.

"I didn't want the pale ale, I wanted the dark, my friend wanted the pale."

The man spoke politely, but Urzahil could tell he was exasperated. Urzahil couldn't keep making mistakes. It would cost him tips. Right now, he needed every copper. He reached over to switch the two tankards. One slipped through his fingers and struck the table, splashing ale on the scarred wood. Urzahil was lucky the whole thing hadn't tipped over.

Later in the kitchen, when he was scraping plates into the slops bucket, he looked around to make sure he was unobserved, then lifted a slice of bread and a chicken leg from a dirty plate for his own supper. Getting something to eat should help wake him up.

The Frog was busy that night, and Urzahil earned as much in tips as he ever had. One more night like this, or two more ordinary nights, and he could walk into the registrar's office with his bag of coins and register for the second term.

After closing, when all the chairs were empty and the pegs by the door were bare, Urzahil washed tankards and lined them up on the bar to dry. He took off his apron, upended the chairs on the tables, and swept the floors. For the first time all evening, he had a quiet moment to think. The tips were good tonight, but what if the next two nights were slow? What if he didn't make his tuition? He hated to think about that. He could ask Allard for a loan, but Allard was a careful businessman and tight with his money.

Emissary: Tuition Money

If he absolutely had to, he could take a coin or two from the cash box. Maybe it wouldn't really be stealing if he paid it back as soon as he could. But he couldn't get caught; he needed this job for next term, both for the tips and the meals. And Allard had always been kind to him, looking the other way when he took a piece of bread from a plate going back to the kitchen and slipped it into his pocket for tomorrow's breakfast, even though it took something away from the hogs.

He stepped behind the bar to look at the cash box. It was a heavy iron casket with a lid, bolted to the floor behind the bar, unlocked during business hours. Right now, it was locked up for the night. Something was wrong. His coat wasn't beside the cash box. He looked up and down the length of the bar. Maybe Allard had moved it when he locked the cash box.

"Urzahil, can you break down the trestle tables?" the innkeeper shouted from the kitchen.

Almost the same words as when Urzahil came in that afternoon, right after he took off his coat and hung it on the peg by the door. Urzahil looked at the door. The row of pegs was empty. He couldn't afford to lose a coat with winter coming on, and he didn't have the money for a new one. Maybe someone had taken it by mistake, and would return it tomorrow.

Unlikely. And even if it were still on the peg, anyone coming through the door could have seen the bulge in the pocket. The coins would be gone by now. There was a roaring in his ears, and he clutched the counter for balance.

"Stupid, stupid, stupid!" He slapped his forehead and cursed himself, but it didn't make it any better.

EIGHT

HEIR RING

JEREMY HOLLOWAY

Jeremy Holloway is a U.S. Army Officer, Louisiana native, and devoted fan of science fiction and fantasy literature. He's currently working on *One Way Mirror*, a novel set in deep space. Many of Jeremy's finished works are short stories he intends to expand into longer pieces. The following selection is one such story, a tale of ancient power and the sepia-toned revelations of a mysterious man of God.

t was packed out that night, but it always was on the bitter days. Days when my family's ring felt especially heavy in my pocket and I could almost hear it whisper, "If only you had done something." Even from the front seat, I could feel the tension flooding the tent. I suppose it's in our genes to establish a routine of complacency, but on occasion a devastating event happens that reminds us of how vulnerable we are. Naturally, we run to our safe place for some divine assurance we are somehow exempt from such catastrophes. *Assurance?* More like insurance. That's what we of the cloth have become nowadays, eternity's insurance agents. As if we actually have a say in whether or not a soul will be spared from eternal damnation.

In truth, I loathe the way people flock to church with their flaky attitudes almost as much as I hate hearing *Taps* being played over the base's loudspeaker. When this first occurred to me, I thought perhaps it was depression resulting from spending eight months of groundhog days in Afghanistan, but my civilian colleagues admit to the same sentiments when hearing *Amazing Grace*. Something I felt at that moment as the band finished its last verse.

We've no less days to sing God's praise than when we'd first begun

With a heavy heart I stood up and walked toward the podium—each step felt harder than the last, but it was nothing compared to the burden of the gold band practically burning a hole in my left pocket. I adjusted it and in true military fashion sucked up my emotions and put on my best face.

"Good evening and welcome to the chapel. This has been one of the most trying months of my career both in the Army and as a Reverend. I thought being part of an aviation battalion would be an easy assignment. Boy, was I mistaken. We've lost many in the previous weeks; fathers, mothers, husbands, wives, brothers, sisters and even some grandparents. But though they are no longer with us, the bible teaches to never forget them or their sacrifices."

Hopefully, there was someone in the audience with enough optimism to believe in this sermon. My own pool of faith felt a bit shallow at that moment.

Think attending a funeral is dreadful? Try doing fifteen in a week for people you've never met. After the service, people tend to linger for a bit to chat before making their way out, but occasionally there's one who'll remain and this was one of those times. I approached slowly, digging up the last ounce of gumption before approaching the young soldier sitting in the last row with his head down.

"Need anything, son? Maybe I can pray for you." The young private had aged thirty years since he'd first stepped off the flight eight months ago. "Oh, it's you, Andrews."

"S-sorry for h-holding you up, s-sir."

"No, it's fine, son. So, you wanna tell me what's bothering you?" Of course, I already knew the answer, but hoped he would surprise me. He didn't. "I-I can't h-help it, sir, been t-trying everything you s-said. But, I keep reliving that day."

I sighed. It had been four months since his brush with death and he'd shown progress in our counseling sessions, but this latest bit of mass casualties must've brought it all crashing back.

"Now, son, there was nothing more you could've done. I've said it, so has the Doc and everybody else."

"It's just that…" He pulled out the Purple Heart medal he'd received after the tragedy which served more as a horrible reminder of that day than as a reward. "Every time I look at this damn thing I feel like—"

"Like what, son, like what? Like you could've done more? Like despite your devotion to the cause, God turned his back on you? Like the failure is all your fault?" Thinking back, I'm not sure if all that was meant for Andrews.

He cleared his throat. "U-um, eeeyyy I-I guess, kinda."

"Well, it wasn't. And eventually you must make peace with what happened and live your life. I'm sure you'll feel much better after going through the hospital in Germany. You're leaving soon, right?" I already knew the answer. In fact, I was partially responsible for convincing his commanding officer to send him back early. I couldn't blame the poor kid, the loss of one's entire squad in one day would be too much for anyone to handle. The best option was to send him away from this wretched place and hope he could heal somehow.

He nodded "Tomorrow afternoon. I-I just… there must have been… maybe I c-coul—"

"No! You couldn't and you need to accept that!" That came out harsher than I intended, but I had heard the whole "shoulda, coulda, woulda" routine one too many times; most often from myself.

"But I can't help thinking if only I'd seen the wires poking out of the road instead of bull-shittin' maybe—"

"That's enough, Private! As a chaplain, I feel this is an unhealthy discussion and as your superior officer I order you to go to the med-station and stay there until it's time for you to leave." He looked at me shocked—hands still trembling around his bible. He eventually stood up and walked out the door, no doubt more downcast than when he entered.

I sat there a while struggling to push away the cataclysm of memories and emotions he'd unknowingly awakened. Images of torched homes and vehicles littered with bullet holes. The wails of my mother, the good missionary's wife, being stripped bare and caned over and over until her pelvis cracked. The taste of dirt and blood in my mouth as I was repeatedly rammed into the dirt, the smell of rotting corpses and human waste while being locked for weeks in a Somali prison. And, the burning rage I felt staring at my cowardly father; a white American missionary exorcising demons in an African hellhole.

The power to stop it all rested in his left pocket. On a whim he could've donned the heirloom and ended the suffering, not just for us but all of Africa. He had real power. Not political influence or money, but true righteous might. Yet, he just sat there looking away, unwilling to assume his birthright and I hated him for it.

I hung around in the chapel for a few more minutes before shoving the skeletons back into my closet and heading to the chow hall for a late-night dinner. Instead of taking the direct route I took the longer path behind the Brigade HQ. In hindsight, I suppose Providence pulled me in that direction. On the way, someone rushed out of the HQ back door. I saw her desperately fish through her uniform pockets for a cigarette. She began nervously puffing as if a doctor had just diagnosed her with a terminal illness. A good shepherd can spot a wounded lamb from a mile away and as such we must nurse our flock.

"Excuse me, are you ok?"

"Chaplain, er, uhh I mean Captain Luria, uh I mean sir."

"That you, Lieutenant Gonzalez?"

"Roger, sir."

"Chaplain is fine. Do you need some help or maybe wanna talk?"

"Negative, I probably shouldn't. You might not have the clearance to know."

"Very well. Have a good night and God bless."

That should have been the end of the conversation which would've granted me the peaceful evening I desperately needed. But there were divine forces at work here.

So, naturally she replied with, "Well, can I trust you to keep a secret. Just between us sir?" while cautiously looking around.

"Always. What's on your mind?"

"It's just that—I've decided to resign my commission."

I did a double take. "That's a bit rash!"

Her voice grew louder. "I know. But... it's just... the mission we're supporting tomorrow night is fucking loco! I can already see what a shit-storm it's gonna be. I don't care if the colonel's sleeping. I'm kicking down his door, march up to him, and pin my butter bar to his face."

"WHOA, whoa, whoa, Gonzalez. Let's take a step back and think this through for a second."

"I just can't believe that mission got approved. It makes no sense."

"Gonzalez, wait a second. Please start from the beginning."

She took a few long puffs. "Sorry, this issue has been eating at me for the past two days. All right, so you know about that botched mission that got all those rangers slaughtered last week?"

"Sure. I just did memorial services for all of them. But I was never told why that happened."

"What was supposed to be a reconnaissance mission turned out to be a terrorist stronghold and… well, the attack helos didn't get there in time… but anyway, they're going in again but this time with 2,000 soldiers. Our Commander has approved the aviation unit's support to escort them with seven Apache gunships with pilots ready to blast anything that even looks wrong, five ambulance birds each with two doctor and two nurses, four Predator drones, and an AC-130 air-bomber will be flying overhead armed to the teeth with—"

"Look, Gonzalez, I know what the bible says about vengeance, but I can't say I disapprove of what the Commander's doing. This is war! Hard decisions have to be made and sometimes it may cost lives. In the grand scheme of things, it's better if it's the lines of the enemy. If you'll recall how Joshua in the Old Testament—"

She blew out a long stream of smoke before throwing down and stepping out the butt embers. "It won't work, sir."

"Say again?"

"They know we're coming."

"How—"

"Ever since the rangers were pulled out, we've had twenty-four-hour surveillance of that area. New vehicles have arrived and are blocking alternate entry points. We're seeing almost no neighborhood residents on the streets except a few 'farmers' suspiciously planting near roads and culverts, and signals units are reporting complete radio silence from that area. That's never happened before." I bit my lower lip, knowing where this would lead.

"So we'll just do an air assault, problem solved."

She took a long drag before answering, "That's what the Commander initially thought, but Azvak valley is way too narrow. Any birds flying in would get either shot up or RPG'ed before they ever landed. So they have to go in by ground."

"If it's the same Azvak valley I've been hearing about, then anything driving through there un-welcomed will get blown to Jupiter. Has anyone asked the commander to lay off until the situation dies down? Maybe try again when the enemy isn't expecting us?"

She took another drag. "No luck, sir, the aviation brigades are heading back to the states next month. It's gonna be at least a few weeks before the new unit gets good enough for this kinda mission."

I rubbed away the phantom buzzing of the ring finger on my left hand and I tried to wrestle away the images of a football field full of body bags.

"But surely the battalion commanders aren't—"

"My warrant officer said he's been in this situation before and that none of them have the balls to say 'No, I don't think we should avenge the rangers'."

"I bet it'll look good on the Colonel's performance review, too."

"Now you see. He's getting his second look for brigadier general this year and this is too perfect an opportunity to pass up. I won't be able to watch when the ambush happens."

My blood had reached its boiling point. One of the reasons I switched from enlisted to officer, joining the darkside, as they call it, was because of my near-death experience. Back when I was just a lowly Chaplain's assistant, a budding lieutenant tagged me to go on a mission that ended up costing the lives of five soldiers, a defense contractor, and almost mine. I was ready to quit altogether, but I decided to go into the Chaplain field after eavesdropping on my boss, a major at the time, as he begged a two-star general to reassign a deployed Brigade Commander based upon reports of erratic behavior linked to apparent PTSD issues. He never received a medal for it but God only knew how many lives were saved that day. Now, it was my turn. But with my ring, I won't be begging anyone.

"This is gonna be a hard pill to swallow, Gonzalez, but I don't think you should resign. You are a good officer, better than most. The Army needs smart, dedicated leaders like you to make it better."

"But sir, I won't be able to live with my…"

"The bible tells us in Matthew 6:25-34 that we shouldn't worry about what is going to happen tomorrow. Who knows, maybe the Colonel will have to scrap the mission for some vehicle or aircraft malfunction."

"You really believe that's gonna happen, sir?" She gnawed on the small stub of the cigarette.

"You're religious, right? All I'm asking is that you pray about it and sleep on it. I'll talk to the Commander tomorrow. Maybe I can convince him to hold back for a little while. God will always make a way, Philippians 2:13-14. This situation is no different. In fact, let's pray right now."

A futile gesture that would only serve to calm Gonzalez until I had time to personally fix the situation. Don't get me wrong, I absolutely believe in prayer, but I also recognize a pearl-eating hog, even one wearing an eagle on his chest. Never in a thousand years would my opinion sway a man like that. Me, a Captain holding down a Major's slot only because the last guy got reassigned for being drunk on duty. The Colonel was a "company man" with ambitions reaching to the highest floors of the Pentagon and across the Potomac. He wasn't here to endure the battle or do what was best for his troops. A modern-day Agamemnon who was here for his position and was willing to sacrifice as many "Greeks" as possible if it meant elevating himself. Luckily for Gonzalez and the rest of the guys assigned to this mission, the Almighty already found a way to solve this ridiculous situation… me!

"Thanks, sir, I'm feeling better already"

"Any time, Gonzalez."

"One more thing sir. I've often wondered about that symbol on your watch."

"It's just a modification of the Star of David."

"Yeah, but I've never seen it like that before."

"According to my grandfather, my family is descended from a long line of Jewish royalty."

"Seriously? That's really awesome."

"Inheriting King Solomon's gold would have been more awesome."

With that she nodded and retreated back inside the HQ.

I continued toward the chow hall and gorged on as much food as my stomach could handle, then headed in for a few hours of sleep. Tonight would be a long one.

At 3:00am I arose fully awake and prepared to perform my real job. With the uptick in rockets hitting the base at night, all defense forces were concentrated toward the north and west parts of the base, leaving the south-east side abandoned.

With the cool mountain breeze on my back, I jogged a mile out until I arrived at a spot right where the crevice point between the two mountains shielding the Southern side of the base parted. A perfect circle of moon light shined on the ground. *Divine confirmation* I thought while unloading my duffel bag of seemingly natural items in preparation for the summoning. Seeing my father's distaste for the family business, my grandpa, an inner-city preacher took great care to make sure I understood every part of the ritual.

"I won't sugarcoat it, son, there are some profoundly evil people who fall through the cracks of the human justice system. Men so despicable that not even the good Lord himself can redeem them; that's where the Luria family comes in. The most important thing to remember when doing this is to protect yourself at all times. Wretched creatures won't hesitate to tear your heart out if you let 'em," he'd say. I cleared all rocks, twigs and loose sand from the moonlit circle until only solid earth remained. Then I dug a small circular trench around and filled it with water from my canteens to serve as a conductor. Next, I poured a few pounds of salt from the chow hall, while uttering some Hebrew chants, to hold that energy. And for the final part, I deposited a piece of canvas paper bearing one of the many cursed marks I copied from the family's written repository of sacred symbols, with a few last-minute additions of my own. Then I sat down to meditate with eyes shut in preparing for the most significant part of this routine.

"This part usually takes me about an hour; the purpose is to achieve complete focus by casting out all nefarious and impure thoughts. Nothing but your just purpose can occupy your mind. If you lose focus, you must proceed no further or risk grim costs," he'd always say, looking me squarely in the eye with both hands tightly gripping my shoulders. Complete mental focus. It was our heritage and duty as descendants of the royal line to be His left hand. Only when my head was empty did I finally don my family's ring and touch the tip of the circle. I willed my spiritual energy in a dome, visible only to those with a sacred sight, over the circle.

All was ready. An interesting thing about us exorcists: everyone knows we have the power to expel evil spirits, because that is the bright side of the coin. Some of us, usually through ancestral ties, can do the reverse. "Hear me, gates of Hades, I command thee to bring forth the minions of Abezethibou to do my bidding."

The cursed symbols moved and expanded until a square-shaped hole, blacker than the blackest oil, was formed. For a moment nothing happened. Then a red flame thundered up, vomiting out three shapeless brown globs before dissipating back into the earth. I watched as the globs began bubbling one by one into various shapes. The first stretched long and formed four giant pincer-like legs, a mosquito's torso, an ant head and scythe-like arms. Once whole, it methodically ran its feelers over the dome, searching for weak points and slashing at possibilities.

The next glob grew outward and began bubbling higher and fatter until it formed a bear's body with four heavily clawed gorilla arms and two lion legs bursting out, complete with a sharp-horned bullhead. Immediately it began clawing, punching, biting and ramming any part of the barrier it could. It even tried to dig its way out.

The third and larger blob remained formless for a while as if it was not sure of what to be, but unexpectedly became a young man in a three-piece business suit. A few drops fell from his elbows and became a high-back leather chair. He took a minute to adjust his collar and straighten his tie before sitting in it. *Curious.*

When the other two realized how fruitless their attempts were, they turned and noticed me standing a few meters away. I began to feel their attempts to telepathically invade my psyche. Though my mind was well fortified due to the meditation, I still felt the bombardment of hundreds of demonic flies attempting to penetrate my thoughts. After this effort was abandoned, they paused and after somehow ascertaining my gender, both transformed into naked women of different races, and began performing various erotic acts on one another. Then they reshaped into males and repeated the routine. At that point I'd had enough and channeled my irritation into energy which the ring absorbed. The gravity inside the barrier increased, slamming the demons, the seated one included, hard on the ground while various roots simultaneously sprouted and restrained each of them. *I've always wanted to do that.*

Another few minutes went by before the two stopped struggling and also changed into humanoid forms. The one in the suit nodded toward the others "Forgive the impudence shown by these of members of my race, but they might behave better if you'd allow us to see your face." I released the roots and walked to the barrier holding up my left hand for them to see.

"This is all you need to know."

The two faceless ones immediately reeled back, reverting to their beastly forms, but a high-pitched warning from the business-suited turned them human again.

"At first we didn't know why this barrier bore such a sting; many eons have passed since I felt such power from a ring." With that he stood and bowed, touching his face to the ground. I released the restraints of the other two who also bowed and in unison cried, "What is thy will, heir of Solomon?"

"You will go to the designated location and claim the lives of those whose hearts harbor only the darkest of intentions."

From my coat pocket, I retrieved a small map on which Azvak valley was marked with a drop of my blood. I placed the map at the edge of the barrier. They responded with an unearthly cry of what I assume was exhilaration and returned to their monstrous forms; the business-suit grew fifteen feet tall and became a dragon.

"Into Hades their souls shall descend. The lives of these men are now at an end," it roared. I pushed more energy in the ring and a portion of the barrier's energy wall peeled off and formed into heavy collar around each demon's neck. I kicked away some of the salt, shattering the barrier, and all at once they disappeared into the night. I bagged up the rest of my stuff and began jogging back to my tent, but, feeling slightly more winded I soon opted to power walk. *That spell took more out of me than I thought. Now for the hard part.*

After finishing off my umpteenth cup of coffee I opened my mini-fridge and extracted an energy drink and candy bar. It had been six hours since the summoning and the ring drained my energy faster than I could replenish it. As a preacher/exorcist assigned to a church in Bronx, New York, my grandpa was accustomed to these kinds of no-sleep, high-stress situations, so for him the burden of maintaining the bridge between the mortal and spiritual worlds was a breeze; for me, not so much. He probably ate a lot healthier than I do, too. At the fifth hour, and 40 pounds lighter, my ring hummed, signifying the return of the hell spawn.

I walked behind my sleep-tent and looked up to see the dragon circling above then performing a downward spiral and morphing back to the man before touching the ground in front of me. *Showoff.*

"It has been done," it said. I punched the tent wall to my left, summoning the Hell portal that immediately sucked in the other two hellions hiding in separate locations, the ethereal shackles dissolving upon entrance. I turned away to leave, but then turned back as the man-demon remained clearly unaffected by the portal's vacuum. "Your task is complete, hell-spawn. I release you back into the void." It stayed there, unmoved, watching as the portal began shrinking away, taking its shackle with it. "I order you…" *cough* "…to surrender your corporeal essence now—" *wheez* "and go back to hell, you unclean spirit." My breathing grew shallower with every syllable.

The thing smiled with a mouth full of razor-sharp ivories and began walking toward me; its hands changed back into dragon claws.

"It seems your power has come undone."

My vision began to blur. The fatigue from a month of continuous memorial services, combined with sleep deprivation and a now-empty stomach had finally caught up with me. Losing consciousness would release this demon from my grip, giving it free reign to walk the earth while still plugged into the powers of Hades. With my last ounce of strength, I pointed the ring at him and screamed, "You 'ave no puwer hu-'ere dem… on. In the na… Nay… name… uv… da… fa, farder—"

"You are mine, child of Solomon!" It morphed into the dragon and charged.

The last thing I remembered was my knees hitting the rocks and the putrid smell of brimstone.

I awoke several hours later to another bad smell and splitting headache. I looked left to see a soldier sitting silently across the room. The brim of her hat was pulled low over the eyes, but her hair bun touched the back of her neck. The uniform was clean, too clean for Afghanistan, as if it had just been dry cleaned.

I broke the silence with "That was close."

She remained silent.

"Too close if you had to intervene."

"We didn't. Though it was kind of a haze, your final act of faith appears to have channeled enough spirit energy to sever the beast's tether to this realm," she said finally, looking up.

"I know how this goes, so allow me to spare you a lecture. I was arrogant, so arrogant that I almost let a hell-spawn loose upon this earth"

"Not just a hell spawn. A prince."

"Impossible!"

"Do we lie?"

"But how?"

"Arrogance wasn't your only sin this day."

"But I was thorough in my meditation—"

"Not nearly thorough enough. The malice you harbor toward your superior found its way into your heart somehow. Nothing less could have beckoned the notice of such a creature."

"Maybe I should have practiced more advanced yoga techni—"

"No. You should learn from your father's example and pray more. Earthly meditation methods are not enough to stave off demons. Only by faith will you retain power over them!"

"I don't like how your kind freely uses your telepathy to denigrate us."

"The effects of your human fatigue currently prevent it, but your excuses are as predictable as the sun. I was not dispatched simply to return you to your quarters but to deliver a message: Such an incident must never occur again, for if it does this world will be plunged into a century of darkness. And nothing, not even the ring's power, will stop it." She vanished.

I sat there re-evaluating my opinion of my father. It must have been miserable to restrain himself while watching his family get brutalized, but it was acceptable compared to the earth-shattering consequences wrought if another progeny of King David unleashed a demon on humanity, let alone a principality. *Maybe dad wasn't as spineless as I thought.*

While still suffering a mild head-buzzing, I arose and entered the HQ building. The large number of personnel zooming through the halls did not surprise yet I strangely had a feeling of newness. Lieutenant Gonzalez rushed up. "Dios Mio, sir, you won't believe what we're seeing in Azvak valley."

"I'll guess that mission tonight won't happen?"

"How'd you know?"

"One of my gifts as an Army Chaplain."

"That praying deal is really something, isn't it?"

"Something indeed." I chuckled as I adjusted my collar and straightened my cap.

NINE

SOLSTICE MAGIC

STEPHANIE GROOT

Stephanie Groot is a Certified Scrum Master who loves fantasy and science fiction. A 2011 and 2014 NaNoWriMo winner, her first book will soon be published. Here she introduces us to Macy, a young girl learning a few of those mysterious family secrets. Every family has them. None quite like this I expect. The novelist Roald Dahl said "*Watch with glittering eyes the whole world around you, because the greatest secrets are hidden in the most unlikely places.*" Stephanie shares one example, with exhilarating effect.

oday marked the summer solstice, Mom's favorite time of year and, she proclaimed, the most magical. The recollection stung and brought Macy to tears until she remembered the open book she held. Fearful of bleeding ink, she dabbed the pages with her sleeve. When her mother's curly script and hand-inked borders appeared unharmed, Macy sighed.

"Mom wouldn't like tears on her recipes," she whispered.

"If you cry while you're cooking, the food will taste bitter," her mother, Tansy, would have said in her voice that rolled like music. Then she would wrap Macy in a gasping-for-breath hug that defied her pixie-size. That's what Mom would have done. Macy turned her head to avoid damaging the book, which was now the only way to be with her mother.

"One day my recipe book will be yours," Mom said.

"When?" Macy exclaimed.

"Starting on your sixteenth birthday, I will let you cook without any help from me because it's important you add your own twist to my potions. When I'm gone, you must remember to use it carefully and treat the book like the treasure it is. All my magic is in it."

Macy said with a frown, "Then I'll never have it because I don't want you to go away."

However, Mom had been gone the past six months, and, just turned sixteen, Macy sat at the kitchen counter, the cookbook in hand. Longing for her mother, she scanned the recipes penned in colors as bright as the flowers in the garden. I'll do everything the Mom would have.

She flipped the pages until a pressed flower fluttered from the book. Mom's blue rose. With great care, Macy touched the petals. That bush hadn't bloomed since Mom passed. The title, Solstice Special, shimmered with a silver outline that caught her attention. Are you helping me, Mom? I can make the rest of the menu around this recipe:

Fresh peas with mint picked with the solstice day dew.

Mushrooms, grown in the shade of an oak tree, sautéed in butter and sprinkled with thyme.

Soup from spring onions plucked from inside a spider's web.

Lavender honey shortbread with candied blue rose petals.

The dessert is Fern's favorite, but I don't have any blue roses so I'll use strawberries. Macy bookmarked her choices and dashed outside.

Squirrels leaped in the limbs of a giant oak that dominated the neighbor's garden and provided shade for Macy's yard. A blue jay sang a raucous call and the sound of someone whistling drifted on the air. Over the fence bobbed a red baseball cap under which lay a nest of gray hair adorned with an oak leaf.

"Good morning, Mr. van der Veld."

Her neighbor didn't answer until he handed a blue jay a peanut. Like the oak on whose roots he stood, Mr. van der

Veld was wrinkled and tall. His back was straight and his shoulders broad. When he smiled, the bushy brows lifted to show twinkling eyes, green as moss. His voice had a rasp like the sound of squirrels scaling a tree trunk. Sunshine, peeking through the foliage, spotted him like freckles.

"Good morning, Macy, you're up early this solstice day," Mr. van der Veld said with a smile.

"I'm gathering herbs and veggies for dinner."

"I have freshly picked mushrooms, if you are interested."

"Thank you, that saves me a trip to the store," Macy said.

"Would you like some peas, perhaps? My vines gave more than I can eat," he said.

"Yes, please, this is my lucky day," Macy said. As Mr. van der Veld left to gather the vegetables, Macy twisted her ponytail. Would Mr. van der Veld think her silly if she told him her plans? Often she had seen her mother chatting with him over the fence. Perhaps she could confide in him.

When Mr. van der Veld returned he carried a basket. The blue jay fluttered past her and landed on Mr. van der Veld's arm, where he leaned over to peck at the container of peas.

At first Macy spoke in a whisper, but as her confidence grew she ended with a rush. "I'm creating a solstice celebration just like Mom used to. First I'm gathering the food then I'll tackle the garden, pulling up the dead plants and pruning Mom's rose bushes, which still haven't bloomed. I'm going to decorate the gazebo with a fountain and Mom's moonstones."

"That is a grand idea. You will make Fern happy and Tansy would be so proud," Mr. van der Veld said.

"Yula will celebrate with us too," Macy said.

Mr. van der Veld's smile faded. "Yula, your mother's cousin?"

"Yes, she's also Fern's therapist."

Mr. van der Veld's brows raised until his wrinkles folded under his hair.

"Yula says she feels guilty because Mom was coming to meet her when the accident happened. When she saw the trouble Fern was having, she offered to help."

"How is your little sister?"

"She's gotten worse. Despite all Yula's help, Fern stopped talking in April." To hide her rising emotion, Macy inspected the peas.

"What a difficult time, I am sorry. Your mother's charm touched everyone who knew her. How is your father doing?"

"That's the weird thing, at first Dad seemed happier, but lately he is distant. He says everything will be all right, but I have a hard time believing that. Fern's nine years old, and she's losing, not learning, skills. So many troubles—that's why I decided to make the solstice dinner. It's my first time using Mom's cookbook. I just want my Dad to smile and Fern to talk." She gulped down a sob. "I don't know why I'm telling you all of this. I'm sorry."

"Losing one's mother is difficult. You're a special girl, Macy. If anyone can bring your family together, it's you. Talking with you reminds me of many conversations I had with Tansy in this very garden. We always shared tips and treats. Now here, take this, I've added sweet woodruff for your May punch." The vegetables and herbs crossed over the fence. When the old man's fingers brushed hers, Macy felt a tingle.

"Watch closely over little Fern, Macy. Make her the special foods your mother gave you," Mr. van der Veld said in a cracking voice. "And please think of me when you dance in the solstice moonlight."

Some of the mushrooms toppled to the ground as Macy struggled to hold everything. She bent over to gather them. When she stood up to answer her neighbor, he was gone.

))) ● ● ● ● ● ● ● (((

Macy hurried to clean the house and start cooking before Dad and Fern came home. The frequent text messages from Dad tracked his busy day with Fern and Yula. As Macy cut flowers, Dad texted about going to an antique store with Yula. After that, Fern must have had the phone because she sent numerous selfies.

Late afternoon, the squeak of the backdoor announced the arrival of her sister with Dad. Fern's happy toes danced across the wooden floors that glowed from Macy's scrubbing. Trying to contain her excitement, Macy waited in the dining room. Her ears followed Fern, who raced through the house.

The sisters looked nothing alike. With a petite frame and wild red curls, Fern resembled Mom. Macy, willowy with dark hair that fell like waves around her suntanned face, looked like Dad. The only feature the sisters shared was their eyes, the color of violets. When Fern clasped Macy, although the little sister didn't speak, her peals of laughter said volumes. Dad appeared moments later, wide eyed and open mouthed.

"It's the summer solstice."

Macy smiled, "I thought I'd lead the festivities this year. Fern gave me the idea after I found her in the gazebo, tangled in dead morning glory vines with slugs in her hair."

"How could I have forgotten?" Dad murmured. He touched the plates arranged on the table. He paused beside a vase of lilacs that perfumed the air. "Your mother would have been so proud. Come look at everything, Yula."

A sneeze exploded from Yula, who stood in the doorway with a downturned mouth and lowered eyebrows. "I'm sorry, but all the flowers irritate my allergies."

Fern eased from her sister's embrace to touch a mobile of prisms hanging from the light over the table. Then Fern dipped her fingers into a bowl brimming with water and floating candles. The sight made Macy's throat tighten.

"The water is my addition to Mom's traditional crystals and flower decorations."

"You're a water sprite, just like Mom always said." Dad smiled as he stopped next to Fern. "Macy, the house looks awesome. You make me so happy."

With a snort, Yula ventured into the room, stopping by a container of hydrangeas and dinner-plate-sized Queen Anne's Lace. She sneezed and blossoms fell like confetti. "I don't mean to complain, but the pollen in here is too much. Can we clear up some of this and get ready for dinner?"

Dad stiffened. "Macy decorated the house for us and I'm not changing a thing."

"You made a wonderful display. I don't mean to complain, but flowers burn my nose." Yula stretched her lips into something like a smile as she embraced Macy. "I'll start the grill for the steaks."

"I already made dinner. Look." Macy waved them into the kitchen. Her excitement infused her father and sister. Dad growled with hunger. Fern flapped her hands and danced to each dish, but Yula rolled her eyes.

"Did you make onion soup, mushroom tarts, and peas with mint?" she asked.

"Yes, I used the vegetables and herbs from Mr. van der Veld's garden," said Macy.

"Is that lavender honey shortbread?" Dad asked as he rubbed his palms and grinned.

Yula pursed her lips while her hands squeezed the shopping bag. "You made quite the spread Macy, but—"

"Great! I'm so glad you like it, Yula."

"I meant to say, think of Fern. Does this food contain all the nutrients she needs?" When Yula nodded, her hair flowed in a pale wave. Macy swallowed. The enthusiasm from Dad and Fern bubbled over, but nothing excited Yula.

"Let's eat," Fern said as she hugged her sister. Dad and Macy gasped at the sound of her voice. Months of trying but nothing had made Fern speak, only humming, hooting, or cooing.

"Okay, Fern. You decided and that's what we'll do," said Dad with tears in his eyes.

Yula opened the fridge and tossed the steaks inside, "Well spoken, Fern. I guess we're eating Macy's gourmet cooking tonight. Wherever did you find such original recipes?"

"Everything I made came from my mom's cookbook," Macy said.

At the dinner table, Tansy's prisms reflected rainbows. The bright sun bounced off Yula's hair while it crowned Fern and Macy with a halo. As they raised glasses of May punch, Macy felt success. Fern's smile and the air of relaxation surrounding Dad said more than words could express.

))) ● ● ● ● ● ● ● (((

Throughout the meal, Macy noticed how Yula hunched over her plate and pushed her food from side to side. When Dad joked, the smile Yula flashed never reached her eyes. The charms on Yula's bracelet rattled as she separated mushrooms from peas. When Yula raised an empty fork to her lips, she caught Macy staring at her. "Yes?"

"I'm admiring your bracelet," Macy said. "The glass ball charms are very unique. Each one holds something different: a rose, a twig with a tiny leaf, and a pebble."

"It's a family heirloom." Yula smashed a pea then set down her silverware. "What a wonderful dinner, Macy."

"Come on, Fern, let's clear the plates." Dad shoved back his chair. "Then we can have the shortbread!"

Yula sprang to her feet. "I'll make coffee."

"Just for yourself, Yula. Tonight, I want May punch. It goes better with this dessert," said Dad.

Only Macy heard Yula grumble, "Have your way, for now."

Cries of rapture from Dad and Fern greeted the presentation of the dessert. The lavender honey shortbread gleamed like gold. Tiny wild strawberries and whipped cream accompanied the sweet course. With care, Macy placed a wedge of shortbread in front of Yula. The woman protested, "I'm not a fan of lavender."

"It's the solstice and I made food that will bring you luck," Macy encouraged. She watched while Yula stabbed a strawberry and dipped the tip in whipped cream. Yula closed her lips around the fruit and Macy smiled.

When the feast came to an end, Fern and Macy finished the dishes while Dad and Yula took a turn around the garden. The adults' conversation floated through the open window where Macy stood wiping the counter. She leaned nearer to hear them.

"Today is a great day, why the long face? Fern talked! We should be celebrating. This is what we've been longing for."

"Fern said two words. I don't call that a huge success," Yula sniffed. "Grief affects everyone differently. She still needs to finish her treatments with me."

"Tonight Fern said more than she's said in weeks. As for the treatments sessions, I think Macy had a better effect tonight than anything you've done in weeks."

"That is so unfair! You're sharing a family tradition of which I have no part. I'm left out of your inside jokes and rituals. Macy knows I can't be around flowers and eat that food. How am I supposed to feel?"

"I can't believe you are upset over a steak dinner. You don't get your way for one night and this is how you act? I'm shocked, Yula. I didn't think you would pout because Macy planned a surprise for her sister. I expected more from you, especially since you are Tansy's cousin. I'm going inside, goodnight."

Macy closed the window when Yula and Dad separated. When he walked into the room, she asked, "Where's Yula? It's time for solstice games."

"She went home." Dad shrugged. "Dinner was very nice, honey. It's the most relaxing moment I've had in weeks."

In the gazebo, the worry lines creasing Dad's forehead disappeared after a few rounds of egg spinning and toadstool tag. He laughed at silly jokes and wove flower crowns. Fern sprinkled flower petals on the gazebo floor.

"Now, let's play hide and seek," Dad said as he ran to a tree and covered his eyes. "I'm 'it' so you two better hide well—20…19…18…17—"

Macy raced through the yard then tucked herself behind the hedge of azaleas. She watched as Fern slipped back into the gazebo.

The bushes next to Macy rustled and she wondered if a squirrel had wandered into their game.

"Ready or not, here I come!" Dad's voice boomed. When the branches around her shook again, Macy peeked through the leaves. A reflection caught her attention. Light glistened off a charm bracelet. Yula! That spoilsport must have sneaked back into the garden, Macy fumed. She reached for Yula's arm, but her fingers grasped air. Macy debated telling Dad about Yula, but her guilt over eavesdropping held her back.

"Found you, Macy!"

Dad's boney knees appeared in front of her hiding space. She stared at his hairy legs untouched by the sun for many months then she moaned. "I thought I'd found a good spot."

"Obviously not!" Dad laughed. "Now, where could Fern be?"

"I saw her go in the gazebo." Macy jogged ahead.

"That is really a bad hiding spot," Dad said. The gazebo was empty except for the fountain nearly encircled and a ring of flower petals that almost lined the perimeter of the floor. Instead of completing the circle the trail of petals turned abruptly down the steps and disappeared into the yard. Macy ran around the structure but didn't find Fern. A search of the nearby shrubs proved fruitless.

"She really tricked us." Dad shrugged then yelled, "All's clear, Fern, come on out."

"Fern, you win!" Macy called as she peeked into the bed of tulips. Her thoughts swirled. She twisted her fingers. "What if something happened to her? Maybe she's with Yula."

"Yula went home. Fern can't be with her." The night was falling, casting the lilacs and azaleas in darkness. Macy ran to the garden shed but the door was locked and no one answered her call. In the house, they raced from room to room.

"Did you find her?"

"No, there's no sign of her upstairs," Dad's forehead crinkled with worry. Macy clasped his hand.

"Dad, I overheard your conversation with Yula after dinner then I saw her in the garden while we were playing hide-and-seek. Maybe she took Fern."

"What? She wouldn't just take Fern, but maybe—I'm heading over to Yula's place." Dad scooped up the car keys.

"Fern would never go willingly with Yula." Macy swallowed. "She might not speak, but Fern can communicate. She can't stand Yula, but I didn't want to tell you because you said she was helping Fern."

"I should have been clearer to everyone. Things happened so fast; I lost your mother, then Yula came, and Fern's problems—"

"Just find her," Macy interrupted him with a hug. She buried her face in his shirt scented with lavender and honey.

When Dad left, Macy fled for the comfort of the garden. The blue rose bushes sat like twigs beside the blooming lilacs. Fern's flower trail started there. Macy collected the petals off the ground. She entered the gazebo singing words of her mother's summer solstice song as she traced Fern's flower circle.

Come into the garden when the spring wind blows and the daylight grows.

The sunlight fades with glory and the night becomes a story on this solstice day.

"Perfect timing." Yula stood on the path with Fern gripped firmly by the arm.

Macy glowered. "Leave my sister alone and go home."

"I've had enough of you running the show tonight, sprite," Yula purred. "Back off. My work here is almost done."

“Let her go.” Macy boiled with anger when she saw the pain and fear on her sister’s face. Her fingers curled into fists that crushed the flower petals.

“This is Fern’s last treatment session with me,” Yula said. “We’re about to get started. This is a private session so no observers allowed.”

“I don’t think you’ll be giving any more sessions, Yula. Take your hands off my sister and get out.” Macy stomped down the steps. “My Dad will be here in a minute so you’d better leave, right now.”

“Make me, sprite. I’m not afraid of your Daddy. And if you stand in my way and you’ll get it worse than your stupid mother.” The woman spat. Behind Macy, the moon broke over the horizon and painted Yula a sickly shade of yellow. The light made Yula’s hair glow and reflected off her bracelet.

Macy froze. “What are you saying? Did you have something to do with Mom’s accident?”

“Ha,” Yula snorted, “I guess Tansy did have what some call an unfortunate experience. She never knew her limitations.”

“You’re despicable. A family supports and loves one another. You aren’t part of my family anymore.” Macy shouted. “Get out of my yard.”

“Blah, blah, blah, you sound just like Tansy. And once upon a time I was your mother’s friend until that wretched elf became careless.”

"Did you call my mom an elf? You need help." Macy said. No wonder Fern wouldn't speak. Yula must have frightened her into silence. Macy risked a glance around the garden to look for a weapon. There was no easy escape route. Maybe she could free Fern with a surprise tackle on Yula, but in a race to the house the woman would out run Fern.

"I'm self-sufficient, thank you. The last time I asked for assistance your mother decided that marrying a worthless human was the answer! She wasted strong magic making you and your sister. How could she believe children from such a union would make our kind stronger? What did that effort bring? Nothing! She put everyone at risk while she got lazy," Yula said.

Macy trembled. Obviously the therapist had lost touch with reality. Fearing Yula would snap, Macy forced herself to sound calm. The sprinkler system sprang on. Water misted the azaleas and lilacs. Macy drew a deep breath, "I don't understand. Yula, why don't we go inside and talk about this?"

"There's nothing to discuss. Tansy's gone and I am doing what she didn't have the strength do," Yula said. With her free hand, Yula stroked Fern's cheek while the little girl cringed. All Macy's attempts of diplomacy disappeared as Fern shrank from Yula's caress.

"What did you do to my mother?" Macy said. A coldness swept over her. In the garden, the frogs ceased peeping and the chirrups from the crickets faded to silence. From the West, a breeze rushed through the garden.

"Wouldn't you like to know," Yula sneered while she twisted Fern's arm until the child wailed. The movement rattled the rose, twig, and stone charms dangling from the woman's wrist.

"Stop it. What's wrong with you?" Macy yelled. She reached out and as the petals left her hands, they changed into spinning blades that soared toward Yula.

Even though she used Fern as a shield, the missiles slipped past the girl to slice Yula's cheek. With a scream, the woman shoved Fern away and grabbed her face. With a shrieking tone that pierced Macy's ears, Yula said, "You cut me! You worthless good for nothing sprite!"

On tip-toes, Fern ran for Macy.

"Are you okay? Does your arm hurt?" Macy gasped as she hugged her sister. "Something sharp must have been mixed with those flower petals."

Fern's pale face almost glowed in the darkness and her mouth moved like a fish. "No, you made magic."

In the garden, Yula stomped. Her fists punched the air.

"Get down," Macy said. This was the weirdest night ever. She ducked beneath the picnic table. "We have to stay calm. Dad will be back soon."

Yula's hair writhed on a gust of wind and Macy swore the tresses were growing before her eyes.

Eyes round as saucers, Fern unclenched her hands and with a clatter, a dozen small white stones scattered over the floor.

"Leave the rocks, Fern," Macy hissed and tugged her sister. Fern wrenched free and began placing the white stones in a circle inside the ring of petals lining the floor edges.

"Please hurry up, Dad. Yula's gone crazy and Fern is having a fit!" Macy picked a petal off the floor and tossed it into the air to see if more razor blades spun out. Only the petal floated to the floor. "Why no razor blade blossoms this time?"

"You will pay for this," Yula roared. With her bare hands, she ripped an azalea bush out of the ground. "You're no match for me."

Fern pranced around the gazebo. Macy snatched at her sister's bouncing feet. "Are you doing Mom's solstice fairy dance? Not now! Get under the table. I'll dance with you later."

Fern spun from Macy's grasp and began to hum a familiar tune. Her little sister motioned for her to sing, but Macy stared in disbelief at Yula, who sprouted a set of fangs.

"No, Fern, not now," snapped Macy through gritted teeth.

The girl's hands waved in a frantic motion that demanded attention. However, Macy only had eyes for the furrows Yula dug into the ground with her claw-shaped fingernails.

"Calm down," Macy begged.

Fern bounced as her feet danced a jig.

"Stop it," hissed Macy.

"Sing!" Fern said.

Macy shook her head.

"Sing now," Fern shouted and, in shock, Macy relented. Half-hearted at first but growing in volume, Macy sang,

Circle of moonstones on the shortest night
Harness the power of love and light
Sing the song and set the charm
To protect the Folk from all harm.

Standing at the entrance, Fern clutched the last moonstone.

Yula howled. The blonde's head twisted and the writing locks shot toward at the little girl. Macy jumped in front of Fern. She pushed her sister to the floor and tumbled out of the gazebo.

Like a whip, the hair smacked Macy with such force she rolled into the lilac bushes.

What is happening? This can't be real. Macy stared at the tresses snaking around her legs. They roped her in a cold grasp. As the frenzied therapist crooked her finger, the strands dragged her.

Macy flung her arms and clutched the trunk of a lilac bush. She pressed herself into the mulch and grass. The sprinkler sprayed her face and she turned her face to her shoulder. That's how she saw Yula marching over to her. *Dad, please hurry up.*

With a toss of her head, Yula removed her rope of hair, but, before the girl could move, she grabbed Macy's ankle.

A scream burst from Macy's throat for the woman's hands burned like frostbite. Pain, like venom, shot into her veins and spread a numbness through her body. She cried out, "Run, Fern!"

In the cloudless sky, a gale whirled in the garden.

Yula pulled violently. Her grip slipping, Macy grasped a branch and shook it with all her strength. With a shower of petals, the blossoms smacked Yula on the head. The lush fragrance swelled in the air.

As Yula wiped the mask of flowers from her face, her grip on Macy loosened. The woman shuddered. With her free hand, she pinched her nose. Then it came. An immense sneeze lifted Yula off the ground. Macy wriggled free.

"You can't escape me," Yula wheezed. She shook her head and her hair cracked like a whip. Rubbing her face, she staggered sideways. Before she took two steps, she spasmed from an explosion of air.

"Thank you, seasonal allergies," Macy muttered. Her escape path from the garden was clear, but the convulsing Yula blocked the entrance to the gazebo where Fern trembled and flailed her arms in a swimming motion.

"I'll save you!" shouted Macy.

"Make magic, Sprite," Fern yelled as she toppled the fountain in the gazebo. A wave of water curled toward her. Macy wondered at her sister's action, as the water soaked her. A tingling sensation erased the numbness cast by Yula. Her toes tickled and her fingers itched.

Neither shaking her head nor rubbing her hands made the pulsing stop.

"Use the water," someone called out to her in a raspy voice.

Water? Macy thought. Water sprite her mother had called her. Now her mother's face flitted before Macy and the word "Believe" echoed in her ears. In the strangeness ruling this evening, maybe using water wasn't a crazy idea. Potions, Solstice parties, and fairy dances? Was Mom magical? There is no such thing as magic.

She closed her eyes and a vision of spouting water like a geyser appeared. What if I tried? I must be dreaming. I'm still in the azalea bushes and I must have dozed off. In a minute, I'll wake up.

With a click, the sprinkler heads directed their jets on her. Water coated her like armor and she felt it on the ground and clouds. Macy fought conflicting urges to either sink into the earth or fly into the sky. A tickle began in the back of her throat. The water blurred her vision, but Fern cowered as Yula staggered toward the gazebo.

"Macy," Fern squealed.

The terror in her sister's voice forced her into action. Macy immersed herself in the sensation. Jet spray, she pursed her lips and spat. A torrent of water struck and Yula fell back.

I am magical. How am I going to explain this to Dad? Mom had to know about this, but she never said anything. And Yula knows it also. Why's she going after Fern? 'Cause she's magical too. In her protective layer, Macy stomped for the platform, but the woman's hand snatched her. Yula's grip chilled then iced Macy's water-gloved hand. Yula purred, "I wanted a fern, but I'll take a raindrop instead."

"Run, Fern," Macy called in a voice losing its power. She continued to struggle. As she scraped the woman's wrist, a glass bauble snapped off the charm bracelet.

"Not sister too," Fern stood with a glowing moonstone in her hand. After drawing her arm back, Fern sent the gleaming stone flying.

Bright as the solstice moon, the stone thudded into Yula's head and, without a sound, she collapsed in a cloud of hair. Macy slipped free. The sprinkler system turned off.

The moonstone rebounded onto the gazebo floor then skidded to a stop where it completed the circle. In that instant, the wind died and the swirling branches swayed to a stop. The full moon beamed over the garden as crickets began their chorus.

"Do you think we killed her?" gulped Macy between hiccups. She rubbed her wrist and turned to Fern.

"Not likely," said Mr. van der Veld as he hopped over the fence. "You need a lot of power to kill someone of her ilk."

"Not you too," Macy exclaimed, "what's going on?"

Skipping and smiling, Fern flung her arms around Macy. She chirped, "Solstice magic."

"This is a dream," Macy said. Fern hugged her then danced over to kiss Mr. van der Veld's cheek.

Mr. van der Veld gazed solemnly at her and shook his head.

"You want me to believe that I'm an elf." Macy stared at them in disbelief. "Which means Yula, my distant cousin, is also magical? Are you telling me Fern is a fairy too?"

"Actually, you're from a family of sprites. But first, we must address what to do with her," Mr. van der Veld circled Yula's unconscious form.

"That's the only sensible statement I've heard anyone say in a while," Macy said. "I'll call the police and get an ambulance."

Fern and Mr. van der Veld both exclaimed, "No."

"After what you experienced, you know I speak the truth when I say Yula is extremely dangerous. No prison in the human world can restrain her." Mr. van der Veld said.

Fern nodded her head in agreement. In disbelief, Macy shook her head. With wobbling legs, she sat on the gazebo steps.

"We need to tell Dad and the police! We can't cover this up. I'm sixteen. Do you think I'll be charged as an adult? Oh my gosh, none of this can be real. Did you give me the wrong mushrooms?"

"Calm down and chew on this." While he spoke, Mr. van der Veld examined each plant damaged by Yula's rampage. He paused to lay his hands on the furrows in the grass. "This attack is not a hallucination caused by eating mushrooms. I stopped your father from driving to Yula's. I put him to sleep on the sofa. He thinks Fern's disappearance is all a dream. When he awakens tomorrow morning, he'll only have memories of a wonderful dinner, an argument with Yula, and games in the garden."

Macy gaped at her neighbor who now appeared younger and stronger than he did this morning.

Mr. van der Veld sighed, "And as for the police, they will never believe you, Macy. How in the world can you explain blades made out of lilac blossoms and a therapist who attacks people with her hair?"

"But, we have to try!" Macy spluttered. "Look at the garden. Dad will see the damage and know something happened."

"Tell him you have moles."

"I won't lie to my dad."

Mr. van der Veld grinned and pointed to a small gray animal digging in the upturned earth. "Now you don't have to lie. That is a mole and it is digging in your garden."

"What do we do with her body?"

Fern squealed in alarm. Macy and Mr. van der Veld jerked around.

"She's gone! Where's Yula?" Macy jumped to her feet.

A shiver rippled his shoulders. "She left; I'm not surprised. Don't worry, that thing won't come back for a while since you've come into your power, Macy. Yula is licking her wounds, for now."

"The voice I heard telling me to use the water, that was you, wasn't it? I don't understand what is going on," Macy whimpered. Fern nestled close and held her hand.

"Yes, I called out to you. I'll explain more, but first can I see which charm you plucked from the bracelet?"

With a surprised look, Macy glanced at her hand. "I didn't realize I still had it," she murmured as she uncurled her dirt covered fingers to reveal the bauble.

In her palm rested the clear ball that held the leafy twig. The gasp from Mr. van der Veld rustled the branches of the oak. He reached out then stopped himself. "I can't believe it." His voice was a whisper.

"You can have the thing." Macy thrust her hand toward him, but Mr. van der Veld shook his head.

"Macy, I cannot. Since you acquired the charm, only you have the power break the spell."

"This charm is enchanted? How do I undo the magic?"

"Break the glass."

"I hope it doesn't cut me," Macy muttered when the thin glass splintered in her fist. By the time she opened her hand, the twig in the charm had grown into a branch, poking out the sides of her balled hand. As she lowered it to the ground, a cloud of leaves blew from the oak above her. The greenness covered the sprouting mass.

The branch writhed until a tall tree stood in the grass. The girls watched in awe as Mr. van der Veld rushed to embrace the sapling. In the man's arms, the trunk rippled and the lithe branches contracted. Leaves and twigs swirled around then compacted onto the pair.

As the mass melted, a teenaged boy clothed in oak leaves materialized. The boy embraced the older man and lifted him off the ground. Their resemblance was more than deep brown skin and moss green eyes. They shared the same expression as they cried and hugged.

"Is he your son?" whispered Macy. When the wiry-haired man nodded, she felt an ache in her heart, but the flower that Fern placed on her knees made her heart race.

A blue rose.

"Where did you find this?" Macy exclaimed. Earlier today the leafless bushes had looked nearly dead.

"Solstice wish," Fern whispered.

Macy caressed the blossom. "I should have made a wish."

"You did," Mr. van der Veld whispered. "Don't you remember what you told me this morning?"

"I said I wanted my family back and Dad to smile and Fern to talk," she said. "But I didn't get my family back."

"You got your family as you know it. And you were given the flower as a special gift."

The lump in Macy's throat choked her. "If your son was in the twig could my mother be in the rose charm? Can you help me rescue her?"

"I think she is," Mr. van der Veld said. He touched his son's cheek then hugged him once more. "I will share everything I know, but we need help. Grab Tansy's cookbook and we'll go to my house to make our plans."

STEPHANIE GROOT

TEN

TUTTLEBEE, THE SCRIVENER

CHRIS ALDERMAN

Chris Alderman is a linguist working on contracts for the federal government. In building worlds around his stories, Chris often leverages his background in formal syntax and grammar to reveal the subtle power that language has in human behavior and culture.

Here Chris presents a tale that defies words, at least any words I know. Ambrose Bierce, famous for his cynical definitions, described loyalty as *"A virtue peculiar to those who are about to be betrayed."* In ***Tuttlebee, the Scrivener***, Chris uses his own brand of Quixotic language to paint a picture of a powerful ruler and his very loyal subjects.

his is the chronicle of the glorious exploits of the once and forever king of all kings, direct descendent of the Bright Sky Wizard, his most majestic Majesty, King Shiny, King of the Sunshine Kingdom, earthly paradise. I, Tuttlebee, Court Sycophant and Royal Scribe and Chronicler, son of Wassledaub the Brown-Nosed, previous bearer of the title of Court Sycophant and Royal Scribe and Chronicler, and direct descendent of the Bright Sky Wizard's cloud-grazing nanny goat, Grondle, set forth herein to felicitously, loyally, and candidly record the most holy endeavors of the Marvelous King Shiny.

This chronicle begins in year 10 of the Mighty King Shiny's benevolent reign. In this year His Majesty summoned a mighty horde of 7-foot tall, elephant-skinned retainers from the distant land of Far Far Away Eastern Jurrjoram, a land legend says grew atop the heap of steaming bowels left after the Sky Wizard slew the Night Dragon. To this day Far Far Away Eastern Jurrjoram still steams from the heat of the Night Dragon's spilled viscera. His Majesty, King Shiny, became wise of treachery in the ranks of his generals and smote them so mercilessly, so resolutely, and so full of holy Sky Wizardly fury, they all burned in the life-giving conflagration screaming of their love for His Majesty and begging his forgiveness. The Heavenly King also brushed away their seed as well.

Tuttlebee, the Scrivener

In year 14, after years of privilege and bounty under the all-seeing gaze of the Earth-dwelling Divinity, King Shiny, His Majesty resolved to exercise his birthright to take 1,000 virgins to his harem and spend his days bringing his celestial light to their bellies. As our Benevolent Bringer of Plenty was harvesting His virgins, a great rebellious mob from the traitorous town of Gronk descended on His retinue, killing many of His Majesty's retainers and causing Him to form a bead of sweat on his brow. Within the week, His Majesty, bringing all his omnipotent Jurrjoram host to bear, punished the town of Gronk in the name of the all-giving Sky Wizard and left it without its existence and planted a royal forest of impaled heads to people the empty waste. Peace and prosperity followed.

In the year 15, His Majesty's subjects complained of a famine, which was very unapparent to our most omniscient King, whose food stores were aplenty, as His birthright dictated. The King, sprouted from a seed sown by the Sky Wizard, rules and possesses all that He sees, as put forth by the Almighty Sky Wizard himself. This message of divine, shiny wisdom was channeled through Haha the Crooked-Headed, who was brought miraculously to sanity by the Sky Wizard's divine light. Thus, by divine law, everything—living, never-living, and formerly-living—was property of His Majesty. A mob of beggars, with no love for their Almighty King, appeared at the gates of the Sunshine Palace, an edifice adorned with beauteous décor from lands beyond the borders of the Sunshine Kingdom, and caused a gory ruckus. Jurrjoram spears perforated the hides of nearly every foul, traitorous heap of low-quality squat that dared defy the His Shiny Majesty's edict "Go, my children, be happy, bask in My benevolence and glory, know that your lowly efforts are for the ultimate happiness of your Earthly Divinity, who brings you peace and plenty." I, Tuttlebee, scrawl these epic words on the bound vellum of those ingrates, whose tanned hides now comprise 1,000 volumes bearing the words of the Holy King Shiny's illustrious exploits and wisdom.

In the years 16, 17, 18, and 19, a great Blackness descended on the land. The infelicity of the boorish classes, their unkindness for our Magnificent King Shiny, drew the ire of the Sky Wizard himself, who took to smiting the curs en masse. When they resisted their punishment, Jurrjoram spears were there to ensure the King's love and justice were apparent. By year 19, Jurrjoram spears were restless at the lack of opportunity to please His Majesty.

In year 20 of the Bright and Shiny reign of the Holiest of Holy, King of Kings, with a divinity and benevolence bounded to the stars and upon which the Sky Wizard was sure to smile, His Majesty wisely correlated a shortage of bread, milk, and honey with a shortage of farmers in the land. His Majesty dreamed of a great victory in the Lands of the Kinkatooks, where farmers and worshippers would prove plenty. He said the providence of the Sky Wizard would deliver Kinkatookia to Him as tacitly promised at birth. He aptly, with Sky Wizardly inspiration, chose to attack on the Kinkatook holiday of the Summer Solstice, when the whole realm would be filled with drink and oblivion. King Shiny the Conqueror set off with his full Jurrjoram retinue, guided by the light of the Sky Wizard, with the wind and sun to his back, and struck the Kinkatook with great fury and vigor. Jurrjoram spears splintered from overuse, Jurrjoram armor and steel rusted from the rivers of blood the Mighty King set loose. I, Tuttlebee, Court Sycophant, Scribe and Chronicler, do say, with all confidence and honesty, I saw the Sky Wizard grin at the victory. Immediately the Magnificent King set all the Kinkatook men to building a lavish palace from the bones and skulls of the conquered which came in great abundance and saw no exhaustion. His Majesty cemented his rule by engorging the bellies of Kinkatook women with His Celestial Light so that they might multiply in His image. The land glutted and prospered.

ELEVEN

A MEETING AT THE BAKERY

THE HOURLINGS

Meetings began in early 2014, starting with a small assembly of writers who wanted to critique and be critiqued. After just a year, the group blossomed to over 70 members, with a full and boisterous gathering each Sunday.

Of course, the great gravity of writing, or even of art in general, is that it's impossible to be objective about your own work. The mind sees a sentence even where the words don't make sense. The heart hears a narrative, even where events are lifeless.

And so an artist has to choose friends wisely. These are the people who will tell you that you're wrong. We chose each other, one way or the other. And we are encouraged. *Encouraged* in the Olde English sense. Emboldened. Made strong, week into week. Like wolves baying to know the pack is near.

For the strength of the pack is the wolf,
and the strength of the wolf is the pack.
-RUDYARD KIPLING

A Meeting at the Bakery

t was the first of April, and the Bread Company was packed. Between the clatter of dishes and the Muzak piped through the speakers overhead, people had to shout to make themselves heard. Almost every seat was taken, and the line at the counter snaked toward the door.

The Hourlings were gathered at their usual place, the long table by the window. They wouldn't have gotten this table at all, except that one of the organizers, a young woman with blond hair and the delicate features of a Dresden doll, had arrived early and claimed it by sitting down with her laptop and spreading out marked-up copies of *The Narrator* to reserve the rest of the spaces.

One by one, the others arrived, opening laptops and hanging coats over chairs. By adding a smaller table at each end and pulling over a few chairs, the long table could be made to accommodate ten, the late arrivals could still squeeze in and find a few inches of table space.

A teenager behind the counter called a number. One of the writers got up and threaded his way through the crowd, returning with soup and a sandwich. He had to work to find room for them between other people's notebooks and coffee cups.

The delicate young woman leaned forward and raised her voice enough to be heard above the background noise.

"I figured out how to get a small tub of opium onto an airplane. They have excellent security at the major airports, but the smaller regional airports don't usually have x-ray machines.

They're supposed to screen each piece by hand, but they get lazy and only do spot checks. If the tub, I was thinking maybe 2 liters, was placed in an inconspicuous piece of luggage, it's unlikely they'd single it out for inspection."

"You mean, like those black things with a handle and wheelies? The ones you see every business person in the world pulling through the airport?" asked a young mother-to-be, her stomach round beneath her sweatshirt.

"Exactly. Put the name of some respectable organization on the luggage tag, something like the Girl Scouts of America or the Humane Society, and the inspectors will never touch it."

An athletic youth at the next table turned and stared at them, then picked up his plate and moved further away.

"In case they do open the bag, the bomb could be in a box labeled *Caution, Live Snakes*," said a man who had more than passing expertise with Python.

"Too obvious. It would be better to put it in a laundry bag full of dirty underwear," said the one the others had voted, "Most likely to go to the Dark Side." Actually, second most. Those romance writers are pretty tough.

"Yuck," said a woman wearing a blue t-shirt with a drawing of a police box.

"No, seriously. I actually did that once. The customs agent had started to put his hand in the bag when I said, 'That's dirty underwear'. He yanked his arm out so fast, it could have put his shoulder out."

"Double yuck."

A busboy came over and began to remove empty dishes from their table.

"Although I'm not worried about the TSA inspector, I'm worried that too many people know about the plan," she said as she searched for a library book in her Downton Abbey tote bag.

"You mean Alex? I wasn't planning to leave him alive."

The busboy's hand paused briefly, and the color drained from his face. He backed away, then turned and hurried into the kitchen clutching the plastic container of dirty dishes to his chest.

"Oh, I liked Alex. Why not have him, say, accept a job in California?"

"That would take too long. I need him gone now."

"Well, you can't just shoot him, you have to make it look like an accident."

"Maybe the problem is the solution," a new writer said. "What if you plant the opium in Alex's bag and send him to Dulles. The dogs will sniff him out from across the concourse. The DEA can hold him for another 3 or 4 chapters without even filing a charge."

"Well that's great, but where am I gonna find another tub of opium!?!" the young woman was loudly exasperated.

Another diner studied the group with a troubled expression, then picked up his plate and moved away. His companion followed suit.

"I'm planning to poison him, probably with ricin. It's easily obtained from castor beans, which you can buy in a specialty garden store. Except maybe for tobacco, I can't think of a better plant-based poison. Does our resident chemist agree?"

"I would never give ricin to another human being," said the strong-willed redhead. "I'd use one of the heavy metals. Cadmium would work… no wait, it's too expensive to refine. Thallium's the way to go."

"They used thallium to assassinate Soviet dissident Alexander Litvinenko. It was successful, too. Don't look at me like that. It's harder to off someone than you might think," said the one rumored to have been with 'The Company'.

"If you give him thallium, he's going to be so f***ed!"

"Bill, shin kick. We're in a public place, watch what you say," said the former agent.

It hardly mattered. The circle of empty tables around the writing group had expanded until they were virtually alone, in spite of the initially crowded conditions in the café. The man in a baseball shirt who'd been seated one table over was standing by the cash register, in whispered conversation with the manager. All the while, he shot glances at the table by the window.

"What if we don't poison him? We could just shoot him and dispose of the body where it can't be found."

"It's not that easy to get rid of a body."

"Yes, it is," said Bill.

The manager opened his phone and motioned the young people working behind the counter into the kitchen. Several diners exited by the door at the back of the restaurant, abandoning their unfinished meals.

A Meeting at the Bakery

"You can get rid of a body if you know how. The police would look for disturbed earth in your backyard or basement. Now, what I would do is bury him in a newly dug grave where the earth is already disturbed, and if the corpse dogs pick up a scent, well, no surprise there."

Blue and red lights played across the walls and tables of the near-empty restaurant. Two police cars parked at the curb were joined by a third, which screeched to a stop at a crazy angle. Car doors slammed and unintelligible orders crackled over the radios.

Heavily armed officers pushed in through the glass doors. The manager met them and pointed to the ten writers halfway down the room, oblivious to their surroundings, waving their arms and interrupting each other.

"Hands up, nobody move!" an officer barked through a bullhorn.

Members of the swat team poured into the restaurant, armored in Kevlar, with nightsticks and handcuffs swinging at their belts. They surrounded the long table with guns drawn and assumed a crouching stance.

Their leader seized the most dangerous among them, a mastermind who'd long controlled the minds of others through direct mail, by the back of the neck and flung him to the floor.

"Eat some floor, dirt bag!"

Another officer pinned him with a knee between the shoulder blades and cuffed him. Seconds after the assault began, all ten writers were face down on the floor, hands behind their backs with the tip of a high-powered rifle against their temple. And each of the writers shared a single thought,

"I wonder how I can use this in a story."

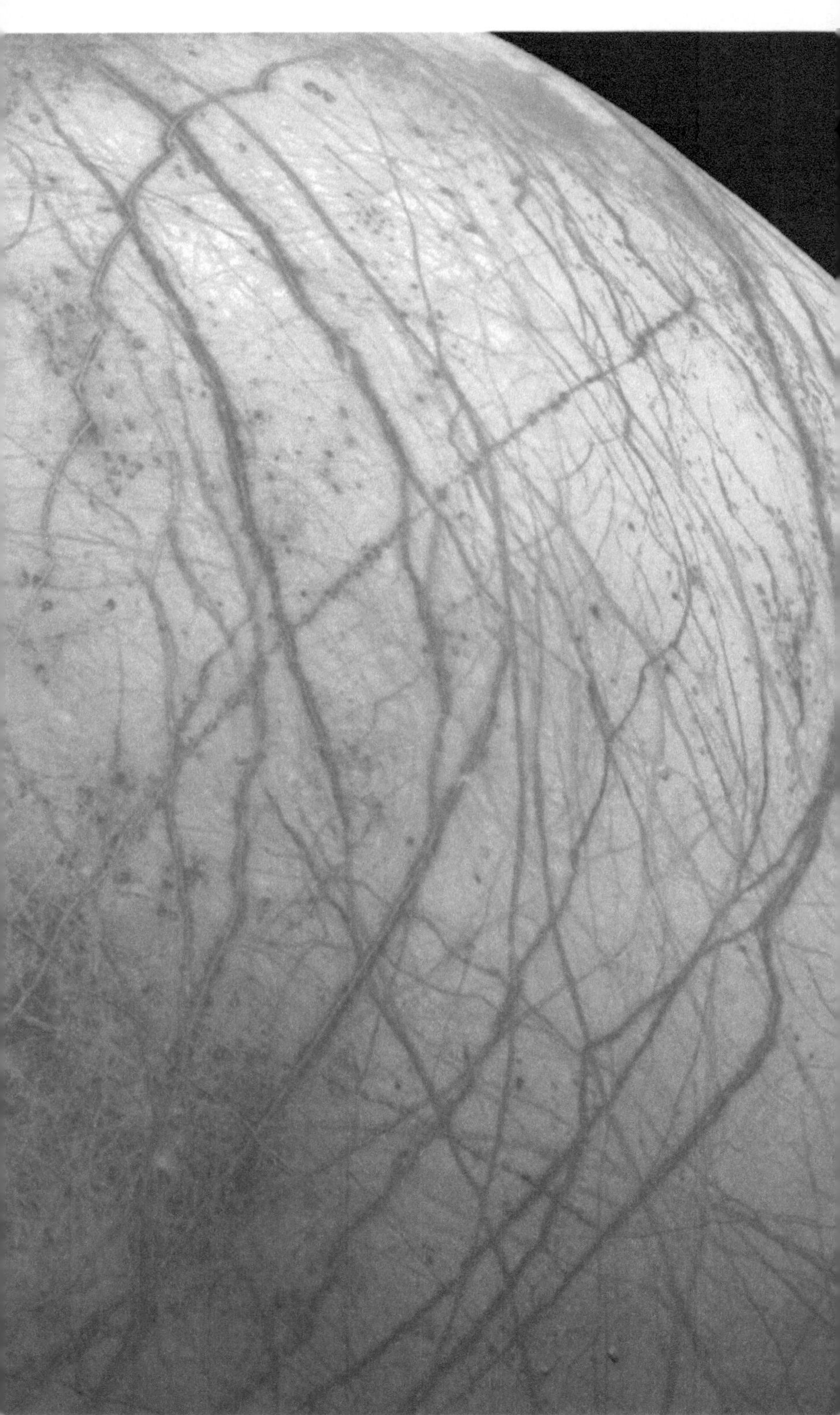

The Book of Other Moons

You know what's weird? Day by day, nothing seems to change, but pretty soon, everything's different.

- Bill Watterson

We have to dare to be ourselves, however fearsome or strange that self may prove to be.

- May Sarton

TWELVE

LOVESICK

KATHARINE REED

Katharine Reed is a native Texan, currently living in Northern Virginia. She works as a technical writer specializing in documentation. Although her academic background is in Technical Communication & Rhetoric, she has started writing science fiction and fantasy. Her most recent project includes a time travel novel set in WWII Germany.

Here Katharine presents that timeless tale of love and sorrow and absolute terror. Turn up the TV. Turn on the lights. We hope you enjoy LOVESICK.

Katharine Reed

As Danni held the cell phone to her ear, she wondered why on earth she had agreed to call him—especially at 1:30 in the morning when she was so tired and painfully vulnerable. Dully tuning out the monotonous ringing in her ear, she let the whole affair repeat over in her mind like a broken tape recorder.

On Sunday night, the last time Jake came to her house, they dangled their legs over the edge of the creaky dock, and the gentle swell of the lake wrinkled like old glass in the wind. The sky melted from blue to violet, and a black raven appeared to hang motionless in the air, strung from an invisible rope. But the moment she ordered him to stay away from her, his anger began to vibrate like a heat wave radiating from his body. As she looked for the last time into his tearful, half-crazed eyes, she knew things could never be the same again.

Her mind snapped back to attention as the ringing came to a sudden stop, and she clearly heard his deep voice. She wiped her sweaty palms on her plaid pajama bottoms.

"Hello?"

"Hey," she replied in clipped tones. "I can't talk for long. Are you sober?"

"Yeah," he replied, a little defensively. "Why can't you talk for long?"

"Because I need sleep," she lied, spouting off another excuse. Truthfully, she just wanted to get this over with. "What do you want to talk about?"

"All right," Jake began, his voice trumpeting a false bravado. Immediately, she began to prayerfully construct a Jake-proof wall around her heart.

Oh please, God. Help me know what to say. Please, God, oh please…

"I've been drinking ever since you broke up with me," he carefully began, "and it's been easy for me to just be mad and not think about how badly I screwed things up. But I did screw up."

Take a deep breath. Don't think about it. You've heard this before.

"I know I took a lot of things from you that you can't get back, but I didn't realize that until today. I know you tried to warn me, but I didn't listen because I thought we were going to get married. You have no idea how sorry I am."

"Look, Jake, I don't hate you, okay?" she insisted, exhaling a weary sigh. She felt her voice sinking into a sleepy murmur. "I'm not mad, and I've already forgiven you. But that doesn't mean we can get back together."

"I know—but I wish we could still be friends!"

"I'm sorry, but we just can't." Her voice was hollow and detached, yet she still tried to be strong. "Not after everything that's gone on between us."

"Why not?"

"You know why," she retorted, swallowing the irritation edging up her throat. Jake had this exasperating habit of questioning "why" repeatedly like an annoying kid who didn't want to go to bed. She had to come up with ten concrete explanations for everything she did before he was finally satisfied.

"I know, but I need to hear you say it," he replied, his voice snapping her thoughts in half.

"Jake..." she paused, surprised by the emotions that collided in her chest. A strange ache constricted her heart like the pressure of tears. "I still have feelings for you. We—we had some good times..."

She let the air escape her lungs and breathed carefully. Her resolve was slipping, and she didn't know how to word things in a way he couldn't twist around. Finally, she closed her eyes and let every broken promise string through her mind.

One time, Jake came over to watch a movie, and they sat on the couch together. Danni immediately laid down the rules: no lying down—it was too tempting. Bad stuff always happened when they lay down together, stuff that made her feel dirty. She could still hear his impish snicker as he sprawled his large body across her lap. All right, baby...

"I don't want to be in love with you anymore," she said firmly, her tone growing stronger with every word. "If we stay friends, neither of us will be able to move on."

"But Danni, I don't want to move on," he pleaded, his voice soft, yet choked with emotion. He tried a different tactic. "Look, I need to be friends with you right now. You're the only person who's ever cared about me, who I can really talk to. Honestly, Danni, I don't think I can make it without you."

The wall was peeling from her heart and crumbling to her feet in large, jagged chunks. She struggled silently with herself, her unspoken words suspended in the air. He knew he was winning. *No—NO! Don't you dare let him talk you into this, Danni!*

"Danni, I know you need me too," he coaxed, swooping in for the kill. "Who else can you to talk to? Who else knows all your secrets? I can be that friend for you—a friend, and nothing else. That's all I'm asking."

"Games, Jake!" Danni exploded before the floating tatters of her willpower had burned to ash. "It's been games this whole time! I feel like we've been playing games throughout our entire relationship!"

She was surprised at the strength in her voice, considering her body was trembling in great, heaving shudders. But he wasn't done yet. Knowing Jake, the best was yet to come.

"Danni," he breathed her name lightly, passionately. She shivered, almost feeling his icy fingers across her skin. For a moment, she let herself remember the Jake she once knew before all the fighting and drunkenness—his soft, brown eyes full of longing and his strong arms wrapped around her shoulders. They had been childhood friends, neighbors for almost her entire life. She fit the sweet, innocent girl-next-door persona to a T. Or at least, she used to.

Her heart rammed into her throat, and it took some seconds for her to swallow it back into place. Somehow, though she knew he was lying, a tender ache threatened to rip itself from her ribs and sink to her feet. Curling her long legs to her chest, she pressed the phone to her ear, struggling to claw out the voice buried deep inside her throat.

"I—I'm sorry," she finally managed, her voice cracking mid-sentence. There was nothing left to say. "I have to go."

"Wait!" his voice suddenly blared. "Don't go! If this is it, at least let me talk to you a little longer!"

Danni sighed and glanced at the clock: it had been almost an hour. If she didn't get off now, she knew she couldn't last much longer. She was crumbling little by little. "No, Jake, I really have to go."

"No, please—don't go!" he implored her, his voice sounding oddly panicked. Danni felt her stomach start to tense as an alarm bell blasted in the back of her mind. It wasn't very often that Jake lost his cool, but when he did…

"Can you come over?" he asked suddenly.

"What?" Danni knew she had shaken him. Jake was losing the battle, and this was his last resort. Careful, she warned herself. What if he's not completely sober?

This wasn't the first time he had been drunk during a phone conversation. Even when he was hundreds of miles away at a boot camp in Louisiana, Danni would wake up to his slurred, throaty voice on the other line, harassing her with perverted words. She had no doubt that he had been looking at porn, and even worse, now he was trained to kill.

"I need to see you one last time," he pleaded. He began speaking in a frantic whisper. "In person—just for five minutes, I promise! You don't even have to say anything!"

Danni remained silent for several seconds, trying to decipher the motive behind his words. What does he think we're going to do if we're not going to talk? She wondered, and this time, the alarm bells rattled in her brain until she could feel them thumping across her skull. There was something panicky and almost crazy about the way he was talking—something almost desperate.

"Jake, you're being ridiculous," she insisted. "I'm not going to walk out of my house in the dead of night to meet you. Alone."

"Please, Danni…" he moaned, his words slurring.

That's when she heard it: crunching. Behind his pleading, Danni could hear the unmistakable sound of boots crunching heavily on gravel. Anger boiled through her stomach, souring her mouth. "Jake—don't you dare come over here!"

"Danni."

With that one word, everything stopped. Her heart seized in her chest; her blood froze in her veins; her breath stalled in her lungs. Her world came crashing down with one gasp.

"I'm already in your driveway."

Her voice lodged in her throat like a block of ice. He stood less than a hundred feet away from her on the other side of that wall. Oh God! Oh God! Her thoughts were a twisted jumble of prayer and panic as she mechanically turned her head toward the window next to her.

"Jake, I want you to go home right now," she ordered, trying to hide the panic creeping into her voice.

As she spoke, Danni scrambled away from the window, feeling her way through the opaque darkness. The tips of her fingers groped for the end of her bed, searching next for the wall and the door to the bathroom. With trembling hands, she turned the knob and stepped into the darkness, carefully shutting the door behind her. A deep, choking sob erupted from her chest as she leaned against the hard surface, sliding gently to the floor. What could she do? If she called the police, Jake would get kicked out of the army! She couldn't hurt him like that, even after all this. Lying down on her side, she curled into a ball, trying to lose herself in a safe corner of her mind.

The small, plastic cell phone was still clutched in her hand, slick with sweat. She brought it to her mouth.

"Jake," she barked, her voice shaking uncontrollably. "Why are you here?"

"I need to see you," he replied. His words were slurring

"No, that's not good enough, Jake," she responded, her voice growing slightly stronger. "It's two in the morning, and you're scaring the crap out of me right now."

Her groping hand found her purse thrown carelessly on the tile floor, and she sat up, pulling it into her lap. Frantically, she fished through the contents: wallet, hairbrush, lip-gloss…finally! Her fingers latched onto her keys, and a quick rush of relief swept over her. She quickly wrapped her hand around one of the bulkiest key chains on the ring and snapped open the top, sliding out a tiny bottle of mace.

"Jake…" Danni coaxed, gently softening her voice an octave lower. "Please. Go home." She stood up and pulled the bathroom door open with trembling hands.

"I'm not leaving here until I see you." His voice rasped in heaving breaths. "Can't you just come over to the window? I could come over…."

"No, Jake!"

She stifled a scream as his bulky shadow abruptly silhouetted in the moonlight across her window shade. Slowly, the two-dimensional figure raised an arm, clearly outlining the shape of a beer bottle in its' hand.

The terrible fury that rolled through Danni's mind at that moment paralyzed her for several seconds. She felt sick to her stomach, and there was a lurching in her bones. Throughout the conversation, she'd suspected he was drunk. Now that her suspicions were confirmed, anger bubbled up in her esophagus, burning her throat. Jake's controlling nature and low self-esteem were a bad combination; now that he was wasted, God only knew what he might do.

Danni snapped her cell phone shut and bolted out the door, her bare feet slapping wildly against the tile. She had to tell someone! The situation was out of her control, and she had to find some way to get it back! Oh, God!

The office lights were on. Relief washed over her as she burst through the door, almost stumbling in her haste to find something familiar and safe. Her mother, who was seated at the computer, blinked up in surprise.

"Mom!" Danni shouted. "Jake's outside my room!"

"What?" her mother asked, her brown eyes dilating in shock. "What do you mean he's outside your room? He's in the house?"

Danni took a deep breath, trying to force her thoughts into logical sentences. She clutched the can of pepper spray tightly to her chest. "Jake's really, really drunk, and he's standing outside my bedroom window."

Somehow, her mother couldn't grasp the seriousness of the situation. She just kept repeating over and over that it was okay; Jake was outside and couldn't get in. Danni wanted to take the woman's shoulders between her hands and rattle her until she got it. This was Jake! If he wanted to get in, he would—end of story.

As the two left the office and walked into the living room, Danni perched on the edge of the couch, ready to take off at the slightest sound. She crossed her arms and tried to forcibly steady her shaking shoulders.

"What do we do?" her mother asked, her fingers clutching fistfuls of cotton nightgown.

I don't know! Danni wanted to scream. *You're supposed to be the adult—why are you asking me?*

Suddenly, the phone in the kitchen rang out with a shrill scream that ripped the silence in two. At first, Danni jumped nervously, but she mustered up enough courage to tiptoe across the linoleum and stand in front of the phone. She hesitated, not sure what to do.

"Do you think it's him?" Her mother whispered over her shoulder.

"I don't know. Probably," she replied, wincing at the piercing clangor. "You answer it." Somehow, getting her mom involved made the whole situation seem less threatening.

"Hello?" her mother threw out in an authoritative "mom-tone." Danni crossed the room and inched over to the door.

"Jake, go home right now," her mother was saying. Danni peered out the round window centered in the wooden frame, almost afraid to look. Her mother's voice floated in and out of her consciousness…

"Danni's not coming out there…"

She clutched her mace tightly, her finger poised on the spray button.

"…I want you to go home right now, or I'm going to call the police…"

A flicker of light caught her attention, and she zeroed in on the spot. It was a tiny cell phone screen, hovering close to the ground. And behind it was a large, dark bulge.

"Mom!" Danni called, her voice ringing with adrenaline. "Mom, it's Jake! I can see him! He's on the ground!"

She came up behind Danni and peered through the window's vacant eye, searching the darkness for movement. They could see a black mass shifting and moving across the grass.

"Oh my God!" Danni breathed in disbelief. "He's coming towards the house!"

Slowly, painstakingly, Jake pushed himself forward by clutching at fistfuls grass and digging into the ground with his feet. He was like a worm.

"This is ridiculous!" Danni's mother spat out, her voice steaming with an old hatred. "He's so drunk that he can't even walk!"

Danni could only stare out the window, her eyes transfixed on the awkward figure inching clumsily across the yard. He was supposed to be her future. Look at him now.

When Jake reached the front door, he stopped. His grimy, mud-streaked hands lay motionless on the damp grass, and a shaft of moonlight illuminated his large lump of a body. Danni wondered if he had alcohol poisoning. She heard footsteps behind her and turned to find her mother running through the house, locking all of the doors and windows. Her white nightgown glided swiftly through the shadows, parting the darkness like a razor blade.

When she returned, they continued to stare into the dark void, past the trees that rose like charcoal marks against the forest. Her mother slowly began to relax, yet she still remained poised, every line in her body eloquent with tension. One minute passed, then another. The can of mace dug uncomfortably into Danni's sweaty palms, and she hesitantly loosened her claw-like grip.

Out of nowhere, Jake sprang to his feet. Danni sucked in a breath as her heart slammed into her ribs, thumping loudly in the silence. Choking on a strangled scream, she stumbled away from the door and ran to a nearby window, her eyes ricocheting across the expansive lawn. Empty.

Oh my God! "Where is he?" she hissed to her mom, who was frantically hopping from window to window as well.

"I don't know! I don't see him!"

"I think I saw him run that way," Danni whimpered, pointing a shaky finger toward the driveway.

Quivering, the two women slowly backed into the narrow hallway. Danni's legs seemed to lock into place, and it was all she could do to drop to her knees, press back into the shadows, and listen past the frenzied rhythm of their hearts.

Tick, tick…

Complete darkness and deadness of sound enveloped the house like a thick downy quilt, undisturbed but for the methodical ticking of the clock above the fireplace. One by one, the seconds passed. With each agonizing tick, Danni felt her heart sink deeper and deeper.

Knock! Knock!

Their heads snapped in the direction of the sound, their minds whirling. Was he in the garage? The garage door was closed! Wasn't it?

Knock! Knock! Knock!

What if the door was unlocked? Could he get in? Danni's mind screamed in terror as panic rolled up her belly.

Bang! Bang! BANG!

The knocking was getting more urgent. "He's banging on your bedroom window!" Her mom whispered urgently. Danni's mind made the connection: he wasn't at the garage after all.

The unmistakable sound of shattering glass echoed down the hall. Danni screamed and clung to her mother's arm. Mom stumbled to her feet and pulled her up, dragging her towards the front door. In their blind terror, they didn't even bother to grab shoes before flinging themselves outside.

The house, located in a fairly secluded area, was almost completely surrounded by woods. Danni and her mother quickly headed for the trees fringing the yard, shrinking back into the foliage. She squatted behind a large oak and fixed her eyes on the front door. It was completely silent save for crickets chirping in the darkness. The summer air was thick and humid, causing Danni's pajamas to stick to her skin. She shifted her weight uncomfortably. Several excruciating minutes passed, but Jake did not appear.

Maybe he had hurt himself when the window shattered and was now sprawled across the carpet, unconscious. Danni was about to suggest that they look inside the windows when Mom nudged her shoulder and pointed to a light glimmering through the leaves. Jake's black pickup truck was parked alongside the house. In his mad frenzy to reach Danni, he left the door on the driver's side open, triggering the overhead dome light. The engine's gentle rumbling indicated that it was still running. They carefully stood to their feet and began to edge toward the truck.

A noise came from the house—the front door creaking open and footsteps on the porch. They froze, darting behind the nearest bushes. Danni's eyes darted towards the truck in front of them, only twenty yards away. If they made a break for it, they might be able to reach the truck before Jake. But try as she might, she could not seem to move her feet, which had turned into lead blocks. Her entire body was frozen with tension.

The sound of ragged breathing cut through the humid air. There was a shuffling noise as he stumbled down the steps, and she peered through the leaves, trying to catch a glimpse. Danni smelled him before she saw him. A horrible stench filled her nostrils, a rank odor tinged with a hint of sweetness. It smelled like rotting meat sprinkled with a few drops of cheap perfume. The smell was so strong that it filled her throat and made her feel mildly nauseous. She covered her mouth and nose with her hand and glanced at her mother, who had done the same.

A bulky shape staggered down the driveway, feet scraping through the gravel. For the first time that night, she had a clear view of him in the ghostly moonlight. He was so close, only a few yards away. In a few short strides, she could be standing next to him.

Danni had never seen Jake like this, even when he was slobbering drunk. He was a mess, blond hair damp and stringy, matted with dirt and blood. His face, deathly pale, wore a blank, expressionless look. She studied him intently, becoming more convinced that he wasn't just drunk. Something was…wrong with him. Jake's hands and forearms were covered with blood, shards of glass lodged in his skin. His right forearm was twisted at an odd angle, and his limbs moved with unnatural jerking motions. There was a low, guttural moan.

Danni looked at her mother with alarm and confusion. "Mom…"

"I know," her mother whispered back. "I think he's sick."

Until they escaped to safety, there was nothing they could do to help him. She and her mother turned away from the pitiful figure and began crawling towards the truck. Danni's cell phone, still clenched in her fingers, suddenly began to vibrate.

She fumbled with it, trying to shut it off, but it was too late: a loud, melodic ringtone blasted across the lawn. Shut up, shut up!

Jake's head snapped in their direction, blank eyes zeroing in on their dark shapes. He lunged for them. Danni screamed and dropped the cell phone. Scrambling to her feet, she aimed her canister of mace and sprayed him blindly in the face. He staggered back as if he were surprised and blinked, apparently unaffected.

Danni just stood there for a second, staring at him with a shocked expression. When he lunged at her, she turned and ran, nearly falling in her haste to get away. She heard her mother's heavy breathing and footsteps right behind her. They clambered inside as soon as they reached the truck.

Danni reached to close the cab door just as Jake caught up with them. His hand, still covered in blood, reached out to block the door. She slammed it shut on his fingers vehemently, expecting him to scream, but he just wrenched them from the crevice in between the door and the cab with an angry grunt.

She shifted the truck into gear, but Jake sensed their intentions and dove in front of them. Danni hesitated, her foot poised over the gas pedal. Even now, she couldn't bring herself to run him over in cold blood.

Taking advantage of her hesitation, Jake heaved himself on top the hood and began to pound on the windshield with heavy strokes. His strength was incredible for someone who was supposed to be drunk, sick, and disoriented. There was a loud, ominous cracking noise, and fissures spread across the windshield. He raised his fist for another strike.

"Go! Just go!" Mom cried. Her voice choked in a half-strangled sob.

Everything happened in a blur. Danni pressed down hard on the gas pedal, and the truck shot forward with a squeal. Caught off guard, Jake slid down the front of the car, wildly groping for something to hold onto. His hands pounded desperately on the hood, but it was too late. He fell to the ground with a shriek as if he had been yanked down and swallowed whole. The vehicle rose and fell with a loud thump and a sickening crunch.

There was a loud pop, and something struck Danni across the face and shoulders. The airbags had deployed. She rested her head back on the seat and closed her eyes. For a still moment, everything was deathly silent. She looked over at her mother, her hands shaking with adrenaline.

"Mom, we just hit him!"

"I know, honey." Her voice was grim, firm. "We need to get out of the car and find a phone. Call the police."

Danni glanced down and noticed Jake's G22 .40 caliber pistol lying upright in the cup holder. Even before Jake joined the army, he had obtained a concealed handgun permit, but she hadn't realized he also kept a gun in the truck with him. Her muscles tensed as she realized how lucky they had been. If he had been thinking clearly, Jake could have used the gun to shoot them.

They waited a moment before moving, breathless with anticipation. She and her mother slowly got out of the car, dreading what they would find. Danni stooped to look underneath the wheels, but Mom touched her shoulder.

"Don't," she said. "Go inside and call 911. Then call Dad and let him know what happened."

Danni obeyed her mother's orders and stood to her feet, turning towards the house. A hand shot out from underneath the truck, latching onto her ankle. She screamed. It yanked down hard, and she smacked into to the ground as the weight was pulled out from under her.

"Danni!" Her mind vaguely registered her mother screaming, but she barely noticed in her blind terror to get away from this thing that was once Jake. She aimed a sharp kick at her attacker and felt her heel connect with bone. The hand released her. She heaved herself upright and tried to get to her feet but stumbled.

Jake, or what was left of him, was squirming out from underneath the car. He was moving quickly, spraying gravel in his frenzy to reach her. One of his flailing hands latched onto her ankle and began pulling her back towards him. Her foot thrust outward, trying to kick him again, but she punched empty air.

She felt heaviness on top of her like a body and Jake's rank breath steaming against her face. Hot saliva dripped onto her cheek. His face was so close to her mouth that they could have kissed. His fingers dug into her arm, and nausea turned in her stomach. Bile edged its way up her throat.

Out of nowhere, a loud crack ripped through her ears, sudden pressure and then dead silence. Jake's body suddenly fell motionless, and she lay there for several moments, unable to move. Mom came running up beside her and knelt down, pushing the lifeless form off her daughter. She was holding Jake's pistol.

"Danni! Oh my God, sweetheart. Are you all right?"

Danni didn't—couldn't—respond. Instead, she stumbled several steps away from the corpse and vomited in the underbrush. Her mother's cool fingers brushed the back of her neck, holding back her hair. After finishing, she collapsed to the ground and buried herself in her mother's arms, letting out a strangled sob. It was over.

THIRTEEN

WINTER ROSES

A STORY OF THE THOUSAND KINGDOMS

DAVID KEENER

David Keener is an author, artist, and public speaker. He writes science fiction, fantasy, and mystery but loves the idea of mashing up his favorite genres in new and unexpected ways. He frequently speaks at conferences and conventions and has conducted a number of well-received writing workshops. He's probably best known for his ***Thousand Kingdoms*** series of connected stories and novels. Find out more at **davidkeener.org**.

Henry Wadsworth Longfellow wrote "*No action, whether foul or fair, is ever done, but leaves somewhere a record written by fingers ghostly, as a blessing or a curse…*" David Keener presents our next piece, a story that contemplates these words. The curse of young love, and the long lingering effects of ancient blood. The beautiful *Winter Roses.*

y darling, are you awake?

I see that you are. I can see your eyes tracking me as I move.

Can you understand me? Try to blink once for 'Yes,' and twice for 'No.'

Well done. I thought I might be too late, my darling … I'm sorry, that was insensitive. My words are clumsy, my manners uncultured by your standard. Here in my mountain kingdom, I have little call for courtly manners and flowery language.

There were … things … that I had to attend to, or I'd never have left your side. I am so sorry about your affliction. I never expected this. I wish, for your sake, that I'd never brought you back to my harsh realm. It hurts me so much to see you like this, so pale and still.

I remember when I first saw you. I'd come down from the mountains to resolve some landholder and right-of-passage disputes with Count Scolatari. He'd insisted on hosting one of his balls while I was there, to distract me from the negotiations I thought at the time.

I'd not have attended, but my own advisors had been hounding me, claiming that at twenty-five I was too long without a wife and an heir to secure the Cragenrath lineage. "Seek out suitable candidates," I was advised.

I was introduced to dozens of hopeful young women at that extravagant celebration. Then I saw you across the hall, holding a crowd of onlookers entranced with your sparkling wit, shaking your raven tresses with merriment. I was lost to anyone else before ever we spoke.

And when I did introduce myself, you made me feel sophisticated, even though I knew I was not. I was thrilled to discover that you had a keen intelligence, and that you had read most of the books that I had read, and many that I had not. Books have always helped my family get through our howling winters.

I was even more surprised when I learned of your modest skills with the sword. I eagerly volunteered to instruct you further in your swordsmanship, a skill that you took to readily, and far more gracefully than I.

I stayed long at Scolatari's keep, and when I left, I asked you to accompany me. I asked you to share my mountain realm with me, to be my wife. I was overjoyed when you said "Yes." It was the happiest I have ever been.

I wish now that I had never succumbed to your charms, because it brought you to this…

I'd rather have had a wistful memory of a long-ago dalliance, than this cruel reality that lies before us now.

When you arrived, I introduced you to all of my family and my retainers. I gifted you with the ring you now wear, a family heirloom of immense value. Everyone was impressed with your beauty, your polished ways, your wit. Everyone was overjoyed to meet you.

Nobody was more surprised than I when you fell ill the very next day. Surely, it must be just a simple sickness, easily abolished. But as you grew weaker, it became clear that you had fallen to the Curse of Cragenrath.

I am young, I know. But I am not stupid. The Curse only falls upon those who seek to harm Cragenrath. I never expected this and, obviously, neither did you.

I investigated further. It didn't take me long to discover your compatriots.

AND YOUR HUSBAND!

I'm sorry. In the state you're in, it's unfair of me to shout at you.

Yes, I found your fellow plotters: the scholarly ex-monk, and your husband, a mercenary from Brylandia. I quickly identified the monk as the weaker of the two, and we broke him within a few hours.

I was appalled when I learned how you studied me. Discovered my likes and my weaknesses.

Guessed at my innermost desires. Your husband, using his roguish charm for extracting information from strangers. The ex-monk, with his talent for research.

And you, with your acting skills. An accomplished stage actress from a far-off realm.

Everything you told me was a lie. Even your love was just an act.

The scholar didn't survive the interrogation. We threw his remains, unshriven, off a cliff. May his ghost haunt the mountains in torment.

And your husband…oh, how I hated him. He had your love, and I did not. But I had no choice in the matter. Honor stands above us all.

For the sake of what could have been, I gave him a fighting chance. We fought a duel. That I am here must tell you that he lost.

I can attest, though, that he fought bravely, and was more of a challenge than I had expected. He even gave me a minor scratch. But I am a warrior from the line of warriors that tamed these mountains. I have been trained from childhood by some of the finest swordsmen who ever lived.

He fell with my sword in his stomach. I could have let him suffer in agony for so long as it should take him to die. However, we lords of the mountains are ruthless, but not overly cruel. I gave him mercy and, for your sake, even buried him in the manner of his people.

The ironic thing is that you and your companions were seeking to steal the treasure of Cragenrath. My darling, you're wearing it right now, the ring I gave you when you arrived.

My ancestor seventeen generations agone was a wizard. He crafted a magical heirloom, an ornate, jeweled ring. Our tradition is to gift it to anyone who seeks to join our clan. Those who intend us harm, die an agonizing and withering death that we call the Curse of Cragenrath. Sadly, the Curse is inexorable once it begins, and the ring can't be removed without the magical backblast incinerating everything in this room.

My ancestor wrought far too well.

I've picked out a spot for you, overlooking the view that you found so stunning when you first arrived. I'll plant our famous winter roses above your grave. They have great white flowers, and leaves so dark they're almost black. Hidden beneath the leaves are the thorns. Treachery hiding underneath beauty.

Strangely fitting, I think.

I'm sorry that it has come to this. I still love you, you know.

Even now, I'd set you free if I could. I wish things could have been different.

Rest now, my darling. The pain will be gone soon.

FOURTEEN

CHEERS

RACHAEL TEUSCHLER

Rachael Teuschler is like Batman, if he wasn't an orphan, worked 9:00am to 5:00pm, was female, and wasn't a vigilante. Aspiring writer, white liar, and careless dancer who paints herself as an engineer by day and a vivacious writer at night. Inspired by reality, fantasy, and science fiction, she aims to mimic and combine stories in order to create something new. Her other nonsensical ramblings include ***Aether***, the story of an astronaut Planning Exodus in an age of immortals, and ***Dreamer***, about a boy's adventure to save his own solidifying soul. Please visit the Batcave at: **rachaelteuschler.weebly.com** for more of Rachael's work.

Frederick Douglass, a social reformer and statesman said *"It is easier to build strong children than to repair broken men."* In Rachael's story, we're introduced to Alexander J. McCarther and his dog Greg. Man and man's best friend, out for a walk on a special day. And we find out what can really be repaired when you have nothing but time on your hands.

Cheers

Alexander J. McCarther decided to take his dog for a walk at the end of the world. The old man grabbed his cooler and his folding chair, and headed to the end of his property overlooking the lake, with his golden retriever.

His children had been fortunate enough that they'd escaped the dying planet on ships to other worlds. His wife had been fortunate enough to go peacefully in her sleep. He had been fortunate enough that they'd left him and Greg alone. As Alexander stood looking at the sun's blinding light through protective lenses, the sun shield that surrounded the Earth began to crack. The Brains of his generation had claimed they'd be able to harness the power of the sun, but they only had hastened its inevitable destruction. The shield was a testament to their failure to remedy that destruction. If only he'd known about it a day sooner. Maybe he could have stopped it, but it did not do to dwell on such trivial things.

The cracks in the sun shield cast distorted shadows across the land as the old man took Greg down towards what were once the Great Lakes. Now Lake Erie resembled a steaming pond with great ships abandoned in the drying muck of the coastline. The ships groaned in the heat, their metal unable to keep up with the rising temperature. Weather had always been temperamental in Ohio but the heat on this day was unprecedented.

The trees on his property took on an orange and brown hue from the glaring sunlight. Their leaves curled, trying to find shade within themselves. Greg strolled right along by his side. His children had intended for Greg to go with them, but Alexander had convinced them to take the family piano instead. Only his youngest, Rem, had tried to fight it. She'd always been the softest of the bunch. No matter how much he'd tried to teach her, she'd never learned the importance of respect. Alexander set his folding chair down beside the remains of the dock and plopped down.

Alexander looked at his silver watch. There were about five minutes left. The plastic of the cooler deformed as Alexander opened it. Cursing, the man discovered that he'd forgotten his Jack Daniels. Alexander frowned, stroking his black beard. "This won't do at all Greg."

He grabbed his watch and turned it back twenty minutes. "Let's try that again."

Alexander J. McCarther decided to take his dog for a walk at the end of the world. The old man grabbed his favorite liquor, packed it into his cooler, grabbed his folding chair, and headed to the end of his property overlooking the lake, with his golden retriever. As he set up his chair, Alexander scolded Greg, "That's the first time you let me forget the Jack. You're starting to go senile, old boy."

His dog barked.

"Yes, yes, you do resemble that remark." The old man chuckled to himself.

Alexander plopped into the chair, his liquor in hand. At least the drink was cool to the touch. The old man savored the sting as it slid down his throat, and he stood by the dried lakeshore looking out. Beside him, Greg was heaving and huffing in the heat. Alexander poured some of his drink into his hand and let his dog lap it up. "Here you go Greg. Enjoy it, you crazy pup."

The golden retriever wagged his tail and eagerly licked his master's hands dry-ish. Alexander smiled at his dog beneath his thick beard. "You know Greg? I really thought I could change fate."

The retriever's ears perked up at the mention of his name. Alexander scratched the confused animal behind his ears till the dog's foot went fluttering with enjoyment. Shifting back into the checked pattern of the folding chair, Alexander smiled to himself. "I'd done it before, you know. Thanks to this watch I've changed my fate countless times."

Alexander took off his watch to let Greg sniff the metal. His watch was simple. Silver with a blue face and Roman numerals crowding its edges. Its hands were silver, as were the dials on the side. His old dog wagged his tail uncertainly, brown eyes glancing upwards at the master. The master just took a sip from the bottle and clasped his watch back on. It was his good luck charm and his best asset.

"Money, women, authority, I had it all Greg, but now it counts less than a ten-second piss. I took the gambling debts of my father and I turned myself into someone. I *owned* this world Greg. I won't let it end." Alexander fingered his watch. It was growing warm on his wrist, a sign that he'd need to go back soon. He snorted in defiance. "Time thinks she can catch up to you. She lives for the hunt. The terror in your eyes as the sky comes crashing down around you, but I've been such clever prey, haven't I, Greg? Always ducking away before that Bitch comes to claim her prize."

Somehow that tickled him. Alexander had a steady laugh that shook his whole body. Greg barked with the master. The next swig of Jack tasted warm to Alexander. He could feel the drink making his head swirl. The heat was starting to get unbearable, as great spidery cracks caused rainbows to fall upon the thirsty Earth, their ominous beauty heralding the end once more.

"You know Greg, I thought I'd have had the same fortune as my father and forget at the end all the awful things I did. You didn't know that, did you, Greg? That worthless gambler died forgetting the hell he'd put his family through. Another lucky victim of deteriorating grey matter. I'm not going like that, Greg."

The old man smiled to himself. "At this rate I'll never go."

Alexander tried to drink but found his bottle empty. Instead, he stood up from his folding chair, letting the weight of the heat and memories cling to him. In the muck of his shoreline, they floated to the surface. The fortuitous heist that won him the watch. That first slip back in time that saved his life from a trigger-happy rent-a-cop. Meeting his wife for the first time while robbing her house. How fortunate he'd been to go back in time to court her instead. Taking control of the Underworld, step by neck-breaking step. The crying of his firstborn. The smell of his wife's orange perfume on his lover's neck and the taste of soy on her lips. The leathery feel of the belt he'd used to teach his children to respect him. The feeling of satisfaction at the confusion on his father's face when he found the old bastard and cut his life support. He was drowning in the heat of the weight of memories. Alexander gasped, trying to steal some oxygen from air that set his lungs on fire. Greg whined in discomfort, and Alexander patted his brown fur soothingly. This was the farthest he'd ever let himself go down this timeline.

"They're weighing in, Greg. The ghosts are coming to see the world end." He felt himself getting faint. His watch was hot on his wrist but it still felt reassuring. He'd watched the world burn a hundred times but never let it hurt him before. It was exhilarating. It was terrifying. A Hell he never believed in was walking his Earth and he reveled in turning back the clock on it. Maybe he'd see someone he knew again if he let it go much longer. The old man toasted himself with the empty bottle. He kissed old Greg on the head. "Cheers, my friend."

Alexander tried to remove his goggles so he could see the sun shield splinter with his own eyes, but their metal branded his hand to the touch. He cursed, struggling to remove them. Greg huddled against his master, scared and shaking. Alexander kicked him away. Finally, the old man freed himself and was blinded by the fiery light around him. Alexander fell to his knees, looked at the sun, and laughed as the trees began to smolder. This is what the end of his world looked like. The smoke made his eyes water and Greg began to bark. He felt the sun blister his skin, cooking him. It hurt. Panic set in. The old man reached for his watch.

"Father."

Alexander turned towards the voice of his daughter and choked on his dry tongue. He could barely recognize her. The Rem he knew was not so tall and alien in the space suit she now wore, but her voice was unmistakable. His littlest girl was standing next to him. The blue light of her helmet illuminated her face. She was older now, at least twenty. The dark hair framing her face practically hid the malice of the grey eyes that glared back at him. Beyond her, an inferno ravaged the earth. The trees, his home, the ships, were all playing out their last crackling lines as the fire engulfed them. Alexander didn't see anything but his daughter through the ashes and the scattered rainbows that fell on them. Beyond her, a jagged rip in the fabric of space time beaconed.

Cheers

Alexander barely registered the pain of his blistery skin popping. It was not possible. She couldn't have a watch? No, that's not how his watch even worked. The watch had its limits. She couldn't be here. She was never here before. She'd left on the ship with the others. This wasn't like the watch. This was different. This was crossing not just time but space as well. What was she?

"Rem?" he tried to croak.

His youngest daughter bent over and picked up something from the ground. Alexander had forgotten about the dog that had been quiet for a long while now. Loyal Greg wasn't moving as Rem cradled him in her arms but he could hear a soft whining. Alexander almost didn't hear his daughter's soft words, "Sorry I was so late, Greg."

Rem stepped backwards, carrying the dog through the rip with her. Alexander wheezed and felt the panic seize him once more. Escape from the pain was right in front of him. The old man tried to scramble towards the crack. He could feel the fire upon him now. Just like the leaves on the trees, his clothes were alight. Reaching out with charcoal fingers he wheezed in pain. Rem looked down on him.

Alexander was confused for a moment. Then he realized what his daughter was: she had become just like him. Maybe her powers stemmed from his own watch, maybe from the genetics he'd passed on to her, maybe from some mad experiment in the distant future. Only one thing he knew for certain. She was not here to save him. Rem smiled with satisfaction as the fabric of space time stitched itself shut in front of him. He was alone with the inferno. For a moment, he stood dumb with confusion. Then the pain reminded him of his watch. Its red-hot glow seared him as it melted the flesh from his wrist. Desperately, he fumbled at the knobs but he'd lost all control of his fingers. Alexander rolled on his back, screaming with laughter and pain. The ghosts evaporated from his shoulders as memories melted from his mind. The sun shield shattered and the world was engulfed. Time had cornered her prey at last.

FIFTEEN

TWELVE-WORD STORIES

JEFFREY C. JACOBS

Jeffrey C. *TimeHorse* Jacobs is a failed Physicist and professional Software Engineer, driving an electric car around the Mid-Atlantic. He assists two local writing groups and a Doctor Who club, participates in EV events, and created and produces Project Kronosphere. Jeffrey's work has been published in *Bleed*, an anthology in the horror genre. Here Jeffrey presents a selection of his 12-word fiction.

MISSION

Where is Pete?
Who's in charge?
What's our objective?
Let's go home!

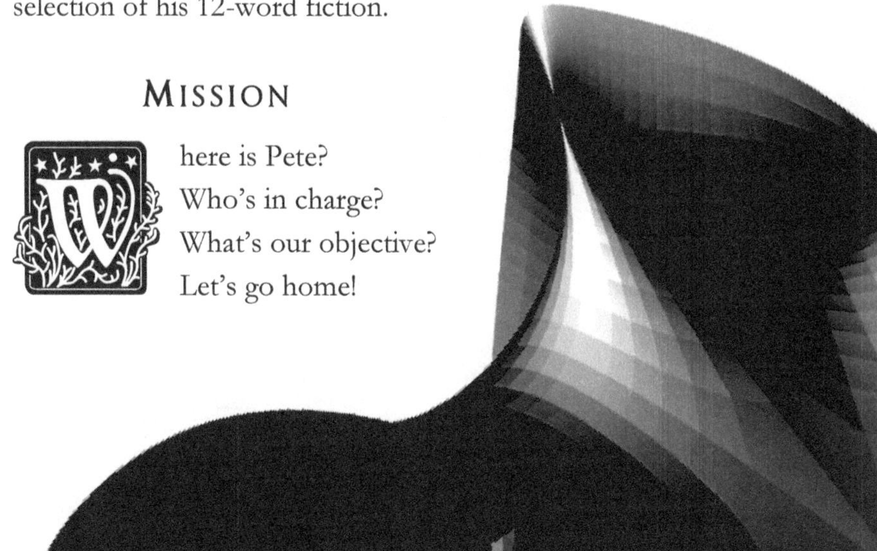

DONNA ROYSTON

EMPTY

All the people,
bereft of love,
bring no joy
to the void.

BRANES

The ship reached
the edge of the
Calabi-Yau Manifold.
It turned left.

SIXTEEN

THE DARKEST EVENING

OOOO OOO● OOOO OOOO

JOHN DWIGHT

John Dwight is a software engineer and artist. He and his wife recently moved into a tiny high-rise condo. At night, something uncanny happens. The city lights speak. They twinkle and blink out coded messages. The greenish lights of a distant farm: "*All cows are gray… on average.*" A vacancy sign near the toll road: "*How can they all be*

the best western?" The angry red beacons on the walls of a prison: "*He is free who wants to be where he is.*"

jfdwight.com.

In this, the last story in our anthology, we follow Sam, a man found guilty for his wife's death and sentenced to Sanistration, a mysterious ritual meant to rehabilitate him. But there is a strangeness here in the story's point-of-view. And a subtleness in the change of tense. This is another one for careful readers.

The story draws inspiration from the work of poet Robert Frost, including chapter titles derived from the poem *Stopping by Woods on a Snowy Evening*. I'll wait a moment while you go off and read it.

Okay then, onward to the end…

The Darkest Evening

Between the Woods and Frozen Lake

○○○○ ○○●● ○○○○ ○○○○

Flora disappeared in late December. *Disappeared.* A pretty word for something ugly. Like she dissolved in a beam of light. Is that how it happened, Sam? I'm dying to know.

I do know *when* it happened, the day, the hour. I've seen the plaster casts of boot treads from the snow, the plates of glass with dusted prints. And I've seen that bloody paring knife, Sam. Smearing the walls of a clear bag marked *Evidence.*

I know you walked together from your cabin on the hill, down to the lake, and ate while the sun set. And you held her hand. I've seen that, Sam. The slender pinkness of her flesh. She wouldn't wear gloves, you said. If it was cold she wanted to feel it.

And you stayed a while, together on the pier as the moon rose. This was the longest night of the year. You stood on the end of that wooden dock and listened to the lake freeze.

"Remember when you would stand up in the boat and sing to me?" you laughed and squeezed her hand. Flora smiled, but hung her head.

The air was still, the pines were silent, and so the simple sounds of ice forming lingered on the night. A wide white crinkling of cold glass. But with that, a moaning too. The restless grunts of the Black Alder. The little boat whose hull was getting squeezed by the lake as it froze.

"It's no one's fault, hon," you said. "The ice does strange things."

You'd gone out the night before, in your little two-person boat and sailed the lake as you'd done many times. And then Flora had fastened the craft to those wooden pilings with big loops of rope. But the Alder had gone astray that night, somehow slipped those moorings, and drifted away from the pier.

"I was the one who wanted to take her out," you said. "I knew the ice was close."

But it was a silly thing to do, Sam. Why did you drag Flora out on the lake, anyway?

"There's no sense in watching it, I guess," you said. "It'll be there till the thaw."

The ice was too thin to get out to the Alder. And by the time the ice thickened, the hull would be stuck. You wouldn't be able to pull it back in. Oh, the spring must have seemed like a long wait, Sam.

The Black Alder's bolts and ribs gave a muffled howl. The mast, wrapped in that canvas sail, tipped and churned as the keel wrestled the ice.

"It'll survive, hon," you said. "We'll get her back with the spring." And you pulled Flora to you, wrapped her up in your arms, nuzzled her neck with your cold nose. Flora had no particular reaction.

A light snow began to fall. And the stars gathered strength in the new night.

"I miss the fire," you said, shuffling snowflakes from your arms and elbows, and you turned to Flora and brushed the fallen snow from her head. She was a lovely thing, but light, breakable. A softness that couldn't be squeezed too tight. Flora had dark hair and eyes, but a rosiness in her cheeks, her lips. She was quietly beautiful, numinal, but melancholy too. There was something sentimental in her smile. When I see images of her in my mind, I feel wistful, almost homesick. And I don't even know where I'm from, Sam.

You pulled on Flora's hands, tugged her away from the dock. And you walked together, careful on that wet wood, back to the cobbled path, and continued on, around the frozen lake. Where were you walking, Sam?

"Not much further hon," and you gestured toward the woods. Flora slowed.

That was a cold night, and you're easily cold Sam, but I see something burning in you here. An energetic fear, an anticipation I think.

"Please Flora," you kissed her hand. "It won't be long, I promise." Flora took a step. Then two more. Her pace became resolute. And she wouldn't look at you, Sam. But she seemed to know. God, that drives me crazy. She was troubled by the weight of something hanging between you. But she held your hand, she trusted you until the end.

The pines were silent as the sons of death. And snow fell on snow, cleaning the page of the land. You walked together, north, on a disappearing path.

Flora never came home.

And you loved her, Sam. I know that. Her musical smile, her lyrical eyes. But she was drowning in sadness. The death of your only son, fearless little Iggy. And Flora's world had become a dirge.

As you walked into those white woods, you wept, Sam. An invisible tear, only the moon and I could see. But Flora didn't cry. She just trudged forward, into the lovely darkness.

And you moved your hand over that pack of supplies and into the pocket of your vest. There you had tucked away a short blade, the paring knife, curved like a steel claw. The same one I've seen covered in sticky red.

What happened to your wife, Sam, in those woods so close to home, on a path you both knew well? Where did you take her? Why was she so willing to go? I'm missing something, Sam. I'd give my life to understand.

WITHOUT A FARMHOUSE NEAR

○○○○ ○●●● ○○○○ ○○○○

You kept looking at the marshal's mask. The smooth black plastic of it. The featurelessness. He marched you into the Secure Sanistration Wing of the Mantis Center for Criminal Correction and locked you inside a small room with white walls and an old metal bench. And all the while you kept looking for some humanity behind that black mask. Did you want him to make small talk, Sam? To tell you about his family before leaving you there to be processed? Well, he wasn't that kind of man. The marshal turned to his affairs. And you sat down on that bench, the paint worn off where stronger men had prepared for their fate.

There was silence for some long time as you waited. For what? Oh, your head must have been spinning. What do we do here after all? Sanistration? I bet you wanted to sleep. So long without a good night's rest. And those soft lights above made all the lines look hazy, the corners and seams and cracks in the brick. Like you'd been locked inside a damp cloud.

Then there was that buzzing. You'll get used to that, Sam. It was the bees. They came through a six-sided hole in the wall. Single file, they buzzed in and formed up around you. There must have been eleven or twelve of them, little creatures, lights fading in and out, sensors reading your heart rate and breathing patterns and bone structure. You stood up, to cooperate I guess, and struggled with your restraints. The elbows get sore don't they, pinned back like that.

The bees left again, through another hexagonal hole and then a door opened into the processing hall, a long white corridor, glass on one side so Judy can watch you. You went through, in small steps, whatever the ankle cuffs would allow.

"Come forward, please." That was Judy. Judy's voice, anyway. You couldn't see her yet. She keeps her distance from people like you. The ones on the way in.

"Stop on the red panel, please. Eyes forward. Do not smile. Do not frown," Judy's voice was crisp like dry leaves. You stepped forward into place, chin up and eyes level.

Click. A pause. *Click. Click.*

"Thank you, Mr. Bellum. You can relax for a moment," said Judy, and then "5-10, 183, 42 and 14 days," she repeated the numbers as she logged them.

You slouched your shoulders and then moved your eyes around the room, past reflections in the glassy wall to the right. There was Judy. You saw her imperfectly, a smear of motion behind streaks of light. She moved, seemed to press something, and the glass became reflective. A silvery mirrored wall.

And there you were, Sam. All 183 pounds. Not exactly your fighting weight. Short hair, unkempt. And dark eyes. We have dark eyes, you and I. Some people like blue eyes, or that magical green color. But I like our eyes. They're serious eyes. You know what I mean, Sam?

"Forward please," Judy moved you along to a white machine with a small nozzle and a red laser projected on the floor.

"Turn your back to the machine, please, and fan out your fingers," Judy said. "You'll hear a short beep, and you may feel a cool sensation on your wrists. That's normal, Mr. Bellum. It will only last a few seconds."

You followed Judy's instructions, maneuvering your restrained hands under the device. But something wasn't right. You didn't hear a beep or feel anything. Your fingers were fanned for a bit before Judy cleared the mirror again.

"Mr. Bellum, can I have you step backward to the red panel," Judy pointed you back, a pretty finger extended sharply to the left. "I need to put a cartridge in the machine." Judy was there before your eyes, but behind glass. You could see her, a small thing, older, with a bouncy mop of silver hair. And she was covering anger too. You noticed that, didn't you. She didn't want to have to change that cartridge with you so close. She liked having that glass in between.

But you were very cooperative. You stepped back onto that red panel and waited your turn, still peering through that long wall of glass. What did you see?

Judy opened a side door, cautiously, slowly, eyes on you. She was breaking protocol here, as she fumbled with that machine, a killer just a few yards away. A killer, Sam. But you were looking through that glass. And beyond, adjacent to the processing hall, was Judy's room, a long console, a comfortable chair, a pot of coffee dripping from the machine. But on the other side of that room, there was a second panel of glass, and through that glass was another hall, not unlike the one you were in. Only that was an exit Sam, a passage to freedom. That was for the ones who survived their Sanistration. And there was a man leaving, on that day, at that moment. How fortunate for him.

He was wearing a gray jumpsuit, disheveled hair, unshaven. He moved an unshackled hand over his foul face. And he was escorted by another man, Lou, a bailiff at the Mantis Center. What did you see through that double glass, as Judy fumbled with the machine?

"Stay in place, please," Judy's eyes bounced between you and the chemical marking device. Her fingers pried at a sticky panel, a fresh cartridge shaking in her hands.

Lou had stopped the man in that other hall. He put his hand on the man's shoulder, an act of kindness, a knowing gesture for a weary soul. And Lou presented the freed man with a box, smallish, white, square on all sides. The man hovered his head over the thing, waiting, waiting. And then Lou removed the lid.

That free man stared, in tired repose, he looked down inside the box for a time. And Lou whispered something in his ear. What was it, do you suppose? Something magical, Sam. But you won't find out until the end.

And you were watching that man, wondering what he had been told. You were staring so intently, in fact, that you leaned away from that red panel, toed those white tiles, just ever so slightly. And then the siren sounded, and red light swept through the room in great arcs. Judy shot her head around, startled by the light and the loud sound. She jumped, and in her haste that machine bit into her, took a chunk of her thumb in its teeth.

At first, she gave a low howl, fearful and wild, barely a human sound. She stumbled and then caught herself, "Stay back!" she yelled, eyes stabbing out into the room.

Judy suckled her thumb and produced a button on the ring of her keys. "Get back!" she waved the device out at you, her left thumb stuffed under her armpit, staining her shirt a deep red, the color of panic.

"I'm sorry, I'm sorry!" you said, but the siren's sound drowned you out. You stood up on your toes in the middle of that red panel. "I'm sorry," you turned your head away.

Judy pointed the device, pressed it, and a burning pain emerged from behind your eyes.

You bowed your head, wincing, your hands still pinned behind you. And you moved back from the red panel, back toward the entry door. "I'm sorry! I lost my…"

Judy pointed the button again. And she barked at you, a wordless command. When the pain hit, you fell over. Still scampering away, knees slipping on those white tiles, fearing Judy, fearing the pain. She walked you back waving a trembling hand in your direction, back to that first door. You cowered there, pushing feebly against the wall, apologizing over and over. Then she bit her bottom lip, chin dripping with blood, and put a shoulder into that side door, returned to the control room from whence she came. And the glass changed back, turned silvery, a mirror once again.

After a moment, the siren faded out. The red light cooled to soft white. And Lou appeared behind the glass, an older man with a round face and smiling eyes. He finished the routine for Judy. You followed his instructions, cautious with your steps. You put your wrists up under that machine again and got your pheromone mark, a scent helpful to the bees. And then off you went.

You didn't mean to hurt Judy, did you? It was just an accident. Is that what happened to Flora? Did you hurt her by mistake? Some folks that come through here are menacing, Sam. But others are just reckless or careless or daft. All manner of killers walk into this place, Sam. But when they walk out, they're all the same.

TO WATCH HIS WOODS

○○○● ○●●● ○○○○ ○○○○

The bees appeared, one by one again, through a hole at the end of the processing hall. You could hear them before you could see them. That torpid buzz seeping through the walls. And they bade you to follow them away. They led you on, in, down a long staircase. The steps began clean and angular, but as you descended stories and stories, the stairs became more carved than created. Lumps of damp rock without rest or railing. The walls went from brick to stone to slabs of earth. And the soft whiteness above gave way to a sharp blackness below. And so you stayed close to the bees, and followed their warm glow down the steps.

At last a floor, it swam up through the darkness like the overturned hull of some sunken ship, resurfacing. And you put your feet down onto it, steady, steady. The bees waited while you gained your balance. Hands are so important for stability, and yours were safely fastened behind you, unable to swing, to steer.

There was a smell at the bottom. A taste really, of mold, of earthen growth. How nice it would have been to put a sleeve over your mouth, to tuck your chin in under your collar. Don't worry, Sam. We wouldn't let you get pneumonia. Nothing interferes with Sanistration. Nothing delays our work.

The bees led on, through what was a cave of sorts, though the dimensions are hard to figure in the utter dark. And the unaccustomed eyes are of little use down here. They just open up wide, gasping for some wisp of light. But in the absence, the imagination paints what the eyes can't see. Fills in blotchy shapes, hideous claws or a drooling maw with teeth. We have that fear don't we, Sam. Of the dark, I mean. Of the things we imagine to be.

At last you came to a stop. The bees disappeared through a small hole in the wall. A locked clicked and turned, and then a door cracked open, the bees tugging on the handle. Slowly, slowly it swung open to let you in. This was your cell.

Spartan accommodations to be sure. You had a look around while the bees observed. We made up the room to be familiar to you, Sam. Just like your home, your cabin in the woods. A little smaller perhaps. A cot, a rocking chair, a fireplace. The wood tones weren't quite right, of course. Your cabin has that nice warm pine. What we had wasn't real wood. It was musty rock, prepared to resemble wood. And the fireplace wasn't real, either. Cold flames. They looked real enough, though. But there was no warmth. Like bathing in a picture of the rain. You really had to use your imagination.

But what about that window, Sam. It looked out on the woods and lake, just like the window in your cabin. Yes, we were buried under hundreds of feet of dank earth. But you could see the land, the pier. The Black Alder was there too, lost in the middle of the lake. You could even hear the sounds of her hull scraping against the ice. And the sun was setting just then. An orange red colored the wet walls. You're welcome, Sam. All the comforts of home.

"Is there a mirror?" you turned to the bees, "I'd like to wash up." You had a couple days' growth on that beard.

The bees gave a calming buzz. And you understood. That you were meant to wait. That something would begin shortly.

You turned around and the bees released your restraints. They tugged on the buckles with clumsy black legs. And then a rush of warm blood came through your elbows and down to your wrists and hands. Did it feel good to you, Sam? On your cot there was a gray jumpsuit, clean and folded, like the one you'd seen on that newly freed man. You put it on while the bees left through their six-sided hole. And then you were alone. All alone. Most of us, in our regular lives are almost never really alone. But isolation can be very therapeutic, Sam. And isn't that why we're here?

You took to your cot, a thin mattress on springs, a sheet, a pillow. Oh the exhaustion. What had it been? Ninety-three days, Sam. Ninety-three days from that first night, the darkest evening, to your questioning, the formal charges, your arraignment, hearing, conviction, and then your sentencing. The constitution guarantees a speedy trial, Sam. You got what you deserved, I suppose.

And in that ninety-three days, you couldn't have slept more than a handful of times. So you were exhausted when you slipped into that simple cot. But still, you must have had a lot on your mind. What, after all, was Sanistration? And of course, you continued under the delusion that you were innocent. A terrible conflict on the mind. And so you began to cry, there in that lonely room. You wept into a pillow crammed under the crook of your neck.

You know what I think, Sam? I think when we cry, we cry for ourselves. For our own loss, or for some fearsome new thing just now tapping our shoulder. It's a selfish act, crying. And that's what brought you here to me. Selfishness. I wish I could say you were crying for Flora, or Iggy, or even for Judy's bloody thumb. But I think you were crying for yourself, Sam. Because you were afraid of Sanistration. Because you were afraid of things to come. Because you were afraid of me.

The Darkest Evening

Promises To Keep

○○○● ○●●● ○○○○ ○●○○

That old red sun had gone down and the night set in. The room was lit by a half moon and the cold flame in the fireplace. A quivering light.

You slept, or tried to. Drifted off for a few minutes at a time. That bed wasn't very comfortable, I guess. And you had become quite an insomniac, Sam. The weight of so much on your mind.

I came to you amid that night. This is where we met, Sam. The door to your cell unlocked for me and I entered. I took light steps not to rouse you, but your breathing was already shallow. You were awake and eyeing me. What did you see there in the dark? A bald spot that looked familiar. Did you recognize my shadow, the shapes of it cast by the fire? They danced across the ceiling, waving as I walked through the room. And I sat there, in that rocking chair, old and wooden. It creaked as I gave it my weight, the sound stabbing out into dark corners. I watched you there from across the room, my eyes shining in the half moon's light. Did you squirm, Sam?

"I thought I had a single," you said, a dingy sheet pulled up to your eyes.

"Don't worry, Sam," I said. "You and I have a lot in common."

And it was your voice Sam, our voice. It sounds different in your head, but you can't mistake it. You knew it was me. You. That we were the same in a sense. Oh God, the fear in your eyes.

You were up without a word. Stumbling away, toward the entrance. And you pressed yourself against that cell door, pushing, searching for a seam at the edges or a switch or a knob. You made a little noise, a groan, weakly. It was the panic escaping your lungs. And your head was cocked around while you worked, watching me, unbelieving. There's something confounding about seeing your own face, without the mirror's lies. Did you think I was backward, Sam? No. We look alike, you and I.

The door did not give way. Alas, it's a prison, Sam. They do their best to keep you in. And so you slowly realized. How wonderful, seeing you slink back into the shadows and take cover beneath that thin sheet.

"Who are you?" you said to me. Your voice came out slippery, like that wet wood at the end of the dock.

I paused for some time, letting the question's echo die.

"Welcome to your Sanistration Sam," I said at last. "It won't be long, I promise."

DOWNY FLAKE

○○○● ○●●● ○○○● ○●○○

"I'm gonna make a snack," you told Flora and hopped up from the fire.

She was working, quiet.

The cabin was made up of a few open spaces, wrapped in warm wood and soft light. It was more room than you needed for two people. But it had been crowded when you were three.

"An apple. You want some apple?"

Flora shook her head. But she gave you a faint smile before returning her attention to the set of black Bayzo boxes on her desk. Flora was an engineer like you. She spent her working life with her mind buried in one of those things.

You plucked up a paring knife and sliced the apple into halves. The fire cracked and hummed.

"I called a man today about a storage locker," you paused, gauging her reaction. "It's big enough for Iggy's stuff." You waved that short blade around the house, pointing toward needles in drawers with orange letters and warning symbols. A refrigerator with racks and silvery sterile hooks and bags for plasma to put off what couldn't be avoided.

"It's in the village though," you said, returning to the apple, halving the halves. "I could take a couple boxes each time I go."

"I thought it might be good to make a little room," you said, wanting, hoping.

Flora's lips only tightened, and so her eyes spoke. What did she say to you without saying? That each day she slipped further away from her little boy. That she was digging in, resolved not to change. To stay the same woman who had pricked Iggy's arm and boiled his blood. The woman who kissed his little fingers as he drifted away. The woman who buried a pinch of Iggy's ashes beneath a hundred different trees, claiming a whole forest for her dead son. Flora felt that any new experience would pull her that much farther from who she had been. And so each day was like the last, as nearly as she could make it.

"I thought it might be good for us," you finished cutting the apple, rinsed the knife, wiped the counter. You like to keep things clean, Sam.

Flora peered deeply into one of those black boxes, tilting it just so, and moving her fingers, twisting, tinkering with something delicate at a distance.

"I'm saving you ***three*** slices," you told her as you walked back to the fire. Crawled up to it with your plate of apple. It was a comfort to you. Some folks like the light or the crackle or the company a fire creates. But you need to feel your skin expand and let that orange in. You love the heat of it, Sam.

"I'm saving you ***two*** slices," you called out, Flora hard at work.

Outside, an easy wind whistled across the window pane. A light snow fell. An inch or two to clean the land. But the winter, astronomical winter, was still a couple days away.

"I'm saving you ***one*** slice," you belted out loudly. And then, inevitably you ate the last bit of apple. Flora began to smile.

You were on your feet again, putting things away, cleaning up. And then you went to Flora, wrapped yourself around her, though she was seated and working.

"I'm sorry, am I in the way?" you said.

And then you put your hot cheek on hers, held her awkwardly, warmed her.

"Come sit with me by the fire, hon. Please?"

Flora smiled weakly. You pulled her up, took her by the hand, guided her to the little love seat in front of the blaze.

And the two of you curled up together, held each other as snow fell by the fire light. You felt whole, Sam. Strong, loving. But in her eyes, her fingers, the ends of little hairs on her cheek, you could feel Flora's fatigue. She was drying out, draining away. A broken cup, leaking, soon to be empty.

SOME MISTAKE

○○○● ○●●● ○●○● ○●○○

"When did Iggy die?" I asked.

You were huddled up in the corner of our little cell, leaning into that fireplace, trying to extract some kind of heat. It had none to give.

"More than a year ago. Spring. Just before spring," you said. "He almost made it to the spring." You were leery of me yet, averting your attention. It's hard to get used to. Your own eyes, your own voice.

"And Flora never recovered."

"Flora survived," you said, "That was enough. For a long time that was enough." You put your hands into those flames, moved your fingers through cold tongues, tried to waft the empty glow out and away from the bricks. No use.

"You recovered," I said, "You made yourself comfortable again."

"Mmmmm," you were thoughtful, becoming very thoughtful. And I began to see images of your thoughtfulness. That's how it works. You were thinking and so I saw memories formed in that mood, frozen portraits from when you were deep in thought.

A first one: you were working inside a Bayzo box. Twisting threads, moving tiny things, melting atoms into place. Engineering something small and far away. And another: you and a little boy, Iggy I suppose, hunched over a telescope. A brilliant sky. Scribbling notes in a log.

This was good, Sam. I was already piecing things together. But I came back, refocused.

"Flora needed help, Sam. She was weak and she needed your help," I said.

"No, Flora was stronger than me," you said. "I needed comfort. But Flora wanted to hurt, and so she hurt. Her grief became a purpose. A cause, not an effect."

As you spoke in wistfulness, wistful memories came to my mind, the snapshots of so many lost days. A young Iggy in the woods, exploring, an old tree underfoot. Flora, in a long blue dress, singing to you from across the lake. Still shots lit by the light of happier days.

"You talk as if Flora took her own life," I said, calculating your response.

"No."

"What if she did?" I said, "What if she turned up in a snowdrift, a note tucked close, frozen to her breast? Would you be innocent then?"

"No…" but you quickly reconsidered, "I'm innocent *now*," you said.

There was anger. You were making this easy, Sam. I saw a picture of your hands, badly cut, knuckles bleeding, torn up by the bark of trees. You had punched them, cried out, mangled yourself over your loss. You wanted to hurt too, Sam. Hurt for him. He was a brave thing. Iggy could have conquered worlds. But he became so weak.

And another image, Iggy in pallor, Flora tending to him. But he stared down that needle, Sam. Iggy was never afraid. He didn't blame anyone for his pain. And you raged inside Sam, raged that your son could be at once so strong and so frail.

These were pictures from your head. Dreams, memories. But I could only see what you showed me. Whatever the snowflakes of your mind made clear, in the moment. And I didn't know where anything fit yet. There was no context, no common thread, no history. I was piecing together your story from images out of place in time. But someone needed to learn the truth. And the next best thing to you, was me.

I was looking out the window at the captive Black Alder, the sun streaming in over the lake.

"Why did you take the boat out that night?" I said.

You gave me a funny look, a defensive squint. "I'm only curious," I said.

"We were feeding the fish, dropping bread down into the water. A last meal before the winter seals them in."

"Thoughtful of you, Sam," I raised an eyebrow.

The ice on the lake flexed in the changing air, and the Alder groaned. It made you wince a bit. Even though you understood that it wasn't real. But the window's illusion, the juxtaposition of the sun and moon and sky inside a deep cave, it was something that the brain knew, but the eye forgot. The fireplace, the scenery, our little cell was full of simulations of some far-away life.

"Ok, Sam. We're all innocent. What happened to Iggy was no one's fault," I moved over the landscape of your emotions, choosing, changing, "But what happened to Flora, someone has to answer for that."

You seemed to get restless here, you stood up on your feet. You were thinking, really thinking. We were both trying to figure things out, Sam.

"You must know what happened," you said to me, pointing. "You must already know," you paused, strengthening, wondering, "Why this questioning?"

"Oh, Sam. I only see your memories as you give them to me. I can't read your thoughts. I don't have a handle to those scenes, no way to recollect them, to cultivate them on my own. I need your help, Sam. Lead me to the truth. Let me understand."

"I see," you said, plodding back to your cot, climbing in under the covers. And then you muttered to yourself, something about truths being in and out of favor[1]. Whatever it was, you'd had enough. You tucked yourself in.

"Come on Sam, I'm asking for your help here," I had lost the upper hand, all at once, and you knew it.

---

[1] Frost, *The Black Cottage*

"I already know the truth. That's good enough for me," you were getting cocky. "I want you to fix me. I want to be cured or cleaned out or whatever you do here. Make me like the guys that leave. Dry and flat and empty. Let's do that, now, right now. Make me a blank page. I'm ready for the treatment."

"That's going to happen, Sam. It's happening now. But I don't do it. That's something you have to do yourself," I said.

"When? How?" your arms out wide. "Tell me what to do and I'll do it. Give me the pill. Hook me up to the machine. I want to change."

"Look at you Sam," I said. "You're so vain. You're all so vain. When you leave here, Sam, you'll have no vanity left."

"Ok," you said, deducing. "I have to rid myself of vanity. This is some kind of Tibetan monk thing. I need to achieve enlightenment and a door will open. It's a puzzle or a riddle or something."

"No, Sam. The truth isn't some kind of trick," I paused.

"I already told you the truth," you were getting frustrated. "If you want to kill me, kill me. If you want to punish me, punish me. But I'm not an open book. So I'm not going to think or feel anything. You can just piece together the little pictures you have in your head, and make yourself a quilt for all I care." You rolled over on the bed and turned your back to me.

"Ok," I said, "ok." I smiled at the back of your head, a dark smile. I was getting angry too. An occupational hazard. "Listen to me Sam, men like you and I lived for maybe a hundred thousand years without a single grammatical utterance. We communicated our pain, our aspirations, our joys, entirely without words. We cried out and frowned and wept so the world could understand us. A small yelp, a grunt, just the lines on your brow. I was made to read you, Sam. What can you hide from me? I know your story, I see it already. All I need is the headline." I was sneering, spitting the words at you.

You must have been afraid. Because I saw the images of a fearful man. A bear in the woods, coming through trees, moving them aside with his great weight. A doctor's eyes behind glasses, reading scribbled notes from a medical chart. Oh Sam, you were bleeding images day and night. It was only ever a matter of time.

And you hated me, cowering under that sheet. I thought you were playing the game, pushing me out of your mind. But then you said something strange.

"Lovers wage an endless battle," you said.

"What do you mean, Sam?"

"Lovers wage an endless battle against the world itself. Marriage therefore, is a wartime pact." It was a quotation. You were reciting.

"What's that, Sam?"

"Something I heard once." You were beneath the sheet, turned toward the wall, wistful. We had already done wistful, Sam. I couldn't learn anything from wistful.

"The entropy of things," you said. "Stars boiling away into empty space, energy dissolving into dark waters. Lovers wage that fight against the world. An endless battle. Flora and I are allies." Your mind was calm.

"Ok Sam, but she's gone. You're the only one left fighting."

And then you turned over to see me, to look me in the eyes from across the room.

"Fighting," you said, wagging a finger, arm snaking out from under the sheet of the bed. And you repeated, "Fighting."

Then you sprang up, and walked to the window, that bed sheet around you like a cape. And you looked out through that illusion at the Black Alder waiting alone, in the middle of the frozen lake.

HE WILL NOT SEE ME

○○●● ○●●● ○●○● ○●○○

"They found a paring knife, Sam." I said, sipping ice water. I was leaning against a wall in our shared cell. But the walls weren't more than slabs of vertical rock. Moisture dewed up on those surfaces making them cool, but slippery too, slimy with some unnaturally green growth. The dawn had gone down to day[2], and you and I had eaten *something.* I don't mean to be vague, but God only knows what it was. Bread? A vegetable of some kind. It seemed alien to me, but I haven't gotten used to your taste buds quite yet.

"They found a knife… in a kitchen," you said. "That *is* strange." You sipped coffee, a white ceramic cup. You were clever, Sam. And smart to keep calm.

"That's right, Sam. But this knife had traces of plastic. What was it? A rope? Did you bind her up, Sam?"

You were silent. Not willing to take the bait.

"You held the knife in your hand, Sam. You had it in your pocket that night. What did you mean to do with it?" I was pulling teeth.

You stood up, turned to me, drew a breath. But then you stopped yourself.

"What, Sam? Explain it to me."

You went to the sink, washed your hands.

"Ok, Sam." I let the dust settle.

You splashed some water on your face. You had given up on shaving. There wasn't a mirror anywhere in the cell. You'd tried the back of the food tray and the bottom of that coffee cup. Even the window wasn't made of glass. And so, with no

---

2 Frost, *Nothing Gold Can Stay*

suitably reflective surface in the cell, your whiskers began to shade your face, a subtle darkening as the day went on.

"You know, they found that same plastic in the fireplace, Sam."

"Mmmmm."

"You wanna know what I think, Sam?"

"No."

"I think maybe you suffocated her. That would have been easiest for you," I said.

You walked across our little cell and sat down in the wooden rocking chair, where I had been not long ago, and you drained yourself of emotion.

"I don't think you're a violent guy, Sam. We're not violent in that way," I said. "You just came to a ledge. And you leapt."

I watched you closely for some clue. But you just closed your eyes, became a bearded stone. You were getting wise to this game.

"But they found blood too," I said. "Drops in the fireplace. And a trail of blood in the snow."

"Mmmmm," you said.

"I'm not sure how that got there, Sam," I said. And I closed my eyes too, searching for the handle to an image I only just borrowed. Trying to remember something I never quite knew.

"A pool of blood in the woods. And then a drop, drop, dropping of dark red in a path that led back to your home. To your cabin on the hill, Sam." I squinted. "A trail of blood, left in the cold."

"How much blood did they find?" you asked me.

I jolted up, away from the wall. My eyes bulged. "They found a lot of blood, Sam." My God, I had a bite.

"But you don't know how much," you said.

"More than a nosebleed, Sam. She didn't stub her toe."

"It might be useful to know," you said.

"Why Sam? They found enough." You were helping me, here. This was some kind of clue.

"But they didn't find *her*," you said.

"No." I sighed, a little defeated.

"Mmmmm."

"Look Sam, you cut her. That we know," I said. "And when you got bloody, you burned your clothes."

"When did I suffocate her? After she died?" You were toying with me.

"Ok, then you didn't suffocate her," I said. "You bound her up with plastic rope and destroyed the evidence."

"Did I carry her back into the woods?" you said, "Where we'd just been?"

"You could have done it, Sam," I said. "We have a strong back, you and I. And solid knees. You could have carried her all that way."

"I guess so," you said.

"You're not convinced." I said.

"It's a nice story," you said. "It just doesn't seem like the simplest solution."

"Enlighten me then, Sam," my arms out wide.

"Mmmmm."

I stood up, breathing through my nose. I was trying to keep my cool.

"You're a smug one, Sam. The killers are always smug," I said.

You just rocked back and forth in that chair, calm as kelp.

"Ok, Sam. You're innocent," I said. "But it doesn't matter now. This isn't a trial. I'm not a justice. I'm not here to judge you, Sam. You've already been judged by the jury, by the law. You were guilty in their eyes."

"Then why the questions?" you said.

"Because I want to understand. I'm your advocate in a way, Sam. I want to tell your story, our story," I said. "The more I know you, become you, the more I can help you heal."

You went silent again. A theory forming. A fear.

"What do you think Sanistration is, Sam?"

"I thought it was supposed to change me."

"It is, Sam. It will," I said.

"I'm not afraid. I want to change."

"Good, Sam. You'll be a different man when you leave here," I said. "I promise you that."

"Mmmmm," you said, becoming quiet.

"But you don't know how Sanistration works," I said. "So you're waiting on it, just like me. What goes on here in this strange place?"

And you squinted through a deep breath. "I'd sorely like to know," you said.

"Ok, Sam. I'll tell you a secret. Let's try a little quid pro quo. You see, Sanistration isn't really a punishment. Sanistration is a price. Your actions put you in this box. And Sanistration is how you pay your way out. In the old days, only time could change a man. Now we have better ways, Sam."

You watched me pace. I folded my arms for effect. "We don't want your time, Sam. We want something better. We want your pride. Your vanity. We want your ego, Sam. You murdered your wife and you could walk out of here tomorrow. You just have to leave a small part of yourself behind."

You looked at me, puzzling. You had your hands in a prayerful position, supporting the crest of your chin.

And I embraced that long silence. We were wading in deep, Sam. I let myself think.

"I've been honest with you, Sam," I said. "Now you help me. Tell me what happened, tell me how you killed Flora."

"Mmmmm, " you said.

"I don't care what you did, Sam. It was just a crime of passion. Flora was suffocating in grief. You only played that out. You set her free."

"I only want to change," you said, rubbing your hands, thumb into palm. "Will the Sanistration continue if you know the truth?"

"I *guarantee* it will, Sam. Nothing stops Sanistration."

"Why would you help me if I'm guilty?"

"You *are* guilty, Sam. And my very purpose is to change you. To—," I paused, "To reconstruct your innocence… retroactively."

"What if you learned that I was already innocent?"

I laughed out loud. A big rolling laugh. You had never seen me laugh before. Seen yourself laugh like that. The percussion of it, the undulation can be ugly.

"It doesn't matter to me, Sam. Guilty. Innocent. Sanistration is non-negotiable. Irretrievable. Even I can't escape what's going to happen."

"What *is* going to happen?" you said.

"Well, Sam, I'm going to dig into your mind until I find Flora. And I'm going to keep hacking my way through your memories until we both believe the truth of your guilt."

But you shook your head. "I loved my wife," you said. "I still do. And you can slice up my brain and eat it with a grapefruit spoon. But our love is the only thing you're ever going to find."

Oh, you were so confident, Sam. I like a little confidence, actually. But it started to get in the way. And this was my cell, Sam. I was in control. I needed to remind you of that.

So here I did what had to be done. All at once, the sun in that window went black. The whole big ball of light winked off, snuffed out like a wet match. And the fire, the fake flames went dark too. The illusions dissolved, Sam. And suddenly you knew the truth. That you were half a mile underground, locked inside the belly of a cave. No lights, no friends, just me, and I had a job to do.

In the utter darkness, I moved to you with speed. I put my face to your face, my hands gripping the arms of that old wooden chair until it creaked, until it cried to be out of my grasp.

"You're a killer, Sam. You're a guilty man." My eyes lit up, an unnatural glow. "Maybe you don't even know it yet, but I do. And by the end I'm going to prove it to you."

The rocking chair began to split at the joints and seams. I felt your legs shaking, your mouth agape.

"Innocent men don't come to me, Sam, and guilty men don't leave." I gnashed my teeth, a beast, an invisible monster so close and so familiar.

And then the chair frame splintered, snapped. You were weightless, out of balance, falling. But before you hit the floor, the sun had bloomed again, bright as before, and the fire had crackled to life. You bounced and jittered like oil on a hot pan. Scurried into a corner, shaking, holding a flimsy plank of wood in frail defense.

But I stepped away, calm again, and took to your cot, feet up, relaxing. And I fell fast asleep to the sounds of your ragged breath.

THE DARKEST EVENING

IN THE VILLAGE

○●●● ○●●● ○●○● ○●○○

"Please be seated." Judge Morgan was young. She must have been in her late thirties. Quite fetching, I thought. But very tough. You should have taken your lawyer's advice and changed venues. It was probably the only good counsel he gave you. At least you would have had more time to put together a defense. But you wanted to be tried at home.

The jury ambled in, took their seats. You watched them walk, faced them, let them see who it was they were about to destroy.

"Ladies and gentlemen, I understand you've reached a verdict," the judge lifted a crisp sheet of paper, her spectacles low on her nose.

Judge Morgan read the jury's statement: "We the jury, duly impaneled and sworn, on count number one, murder in the second degree, upon our oaths do find the defendant, Samuel J. Bellum… guilty."

Don't you love how they bury the lead on a statement like that? There's a lot to weed through before they tell you what you really want to know. *Guilty.*

And you knew it was coming, Sam. The jury had been clear. They didn't need to see a body. You left so much evidence. The jury was convinced a murder took place, and the trail of Flora's blood led literally to your door. Still, you sat down with the weight of it, Sam. And wept for yourself. For the price you would have to pay.

"Stay firm, Sammy," your lawyer put his hand on your shoulder. Miller Redman had practiced law in Somerset County for nearly 60 years. And so he made easy claim to more ill-conceived defenses and bungled cases than anyone else in the long history of the state of Maine. Miller Redman was a bad lawyer, Sam. Only a guilty man would hire him.

You stood again as the jury filed out. Their work was done. They were all going back to their lives. And you would stay and be sentenced. Swift justice, the law of the land.

"I'm prepared to sentence the offendant at this time," Judge Morgan said. "Would the defense like to make a statement?"

There was a long silence before Miller Redman realized the judge was talking to him. But he just shook his head. There was really nothing to say.

"In a case like this, the law limits my actions in sentencing," Judge Morgan said, mulling. "But I would afford the offendant some level of leniency if he would lead authorities to his wife's body."

Miller leaned to you, ready to whisper some legal wisdom in your ear. But you had already begun to speak.

"I'm innocent, Your Honor." Your voice came from a deep breath, exhausted. "I don't know where my wife is."

Judge Morgan looked down on you from behind the bench, made of red oak and Kevlar. You met her eyes. She seemed to want another option. But you were so stubborn, Sam. What choice did you give her? What other choice did she have?

"Samuel Bellum, you've been found guilty of murder in the second degree." Judge Morgan's voice became deep and wide, like the barking of a hound. She knew at least, the gravity of her words.

"Being that you were born on or after May 15th of the year 468 in the New Common Era, this court recommends immediate and total Sanistration of the offendant and remands him to the care and custody of the local Marshal service to carry out his sentence." Another mouthful. I love that about justice. What a machine. What a lazy, feckless, tedious, powerful machine.

Exhausted by the trial and the verdict and the sentencing, you collapsed into your chair, closed your eyes, and waited for the marshals in smooth black masks to arrive.

BEFORE I SLEEP

○●●● ○●●● ○●○● ○●○●

"You're just going to wear yourself out Sam," I said.

I was giving you good advice. You were balancing on one foot, trying hard to stay awake.

"I don't know what's gotten into you Sam," I knew exactly what had gotten into you.

"Ok," you said. You were gulping the last of your black coffee and eyeing that window. The illusion of light had become all the more disturbing, since I'd shown you the truth of the dark.

"You're afraid, Sam" I said. "Everyone becomes afraid. You know why?"

"Uhuh," you said. You were rocking in place, swaying, like one of those silent pines.

"All these men, these killers. They love themselves. You have to love yourself to kill, Sam."

"Okuh," you said, pinching your own arm, grinding flesh between your knuckles. It looked like it hurt.

"But then they see me. The angel of death with a familiar face. It shakes them. It breaks them, Sam. Because how can they love themselves if they fear their own voice, their own eyes."

"Urrrr," you said.

"That's when the real dread sets in, Sam. When you fall out of love with yourself. When you start to hate your own hands, your own breath, your own stubbly face."

"Mmm Pmm," you said. You were pushing your cheek into the bare metal frame of the cot. Just to feel something cold, I suppose.

"Why don't you get some rest, Sam? How much longer can you really hold out?"

"Hmm Hmm," you said. You were gnawing your own cheeks, on the inside. There was red on your lips. You were fighting to stay awake.

"I'm going to see what you don't want me to see, Sam."

"Nnnnn," you said.

"And then this can be over. Wouldn't that be good?" I was soothing.

"Nuuuu," you said.

"What, Sam?" I said. "What are you afraid of?"

"You-won't-need-me-then," your words smeared together on tired breath.

"Well," I said, "two of us *is* one too many."

"You're-gonna-replace-me," your eyelids fighting for air.

"Oh Sam," I said. "You worry too much."

"Ffff," you said. You were leaning up against the window. Listening to the Black Alder moan. The light of that false star warmed your cheek. A softening calm.

"But…" I lingered on the thought, "I suppose the world doesn't need us both, Sam."

"Sssss," you said.

"I mean, what did you think, that we would grow old together?"

"Vvvvv," you said, on your feet, drifting, drifting.

"Show me, Sam. Show me who I am."

"Zzzzz," you said, lifting, floating, sailing away into sleep.

Think It Queer

○●●● ●●●● ○●○● ○●○●

The swollen moon swims from dark to day. A land born in space. And the lifeless face of some distant sea.

The eager moon fills the sky. A deep thing rising. The window panes ache, bending with a lifeless weight.

The angry moon cracks the walls. A splintering. The letting of gray veins. A lifeless desert lost grain by grain.

The rabid moon eats the floors. Gorges on halls and milky blood. Chews the lifeless cud of Brahman as she turns.

I Think I Know

●●●● ●●●● ○●○● ○●○●

"Show me her lifelessness, Sam." I was over you, on the hard slab of ground. I had cradled you down. You saw my face as you came to.

"Show me her lifeless body, Sam. Show me her lifeless eyes."

You began to squirm, you rolled out from under my legs and huddled back on a dirty wall.

"Show me a little more, Sam. Let me see her naked lifelessness. Show me her final form." I was billowing zeal.

You cowered again. Pushing against the rock walls, pounding a fist on the floor. But there was no one coming. You and I were alone.

"I saw you in the woods," I said. "A snapshot lit by the moon. I saw that paring knife, Sam. And Flora's blood. A trail of drops in the snow. And your hands were soaked, Sam. Painted in Flora's thick red life."

You were too smart to talk, but you couldn't keep me out.

"There were tracks in the snow, and a trail of blood. It was already done, Sam. You had hurt her and then you let her run. Clever, easy that way. That was a clue before. You didn't carry her, you let her go. She ran into the woods. It was so simple, Sam."

You turned on the water in that small sink and dowsed yourself.

"You followed her tracks to that pool of blood. Was she dead then, Sam? Did you drag her away? Had you already dug the hole? Oh Sam, this was premeditated! I knew you were too clever to leave things to chance. You made a plan, Sam. That's what an engineer would do."

I was giddy, a broad and twisted smile. You paced and dried your face and banged a fist on the door you had come through just yesterday. "Coffee!" you yelled to the bees far away.

"The secret sits in the middle [3], Sam," and I was approaching from all sides.

You moved back to the fire. For comfort, for sanity somehow, shaking. Grasping the flames for warmth.

"I'm innocent," you said, a whimper.

"It doesn't matter, Sam. I need to know what happened, and we're almost there. Soon you'll crack open like an egg and you'll begin to bleed the truth. I'll finally understand, Sam. Soon we'll be at the end."

You put your head in your hands.

"You know what you have to do, Sam. Show me. Recreate it. Make it happen again. Here in this cell. Read between the

---

[3] Robert Frost, *The Secret Sits*

lines, Sam. Words aren't enough. I need to experience the truth of it. That's how you get clean." I was glowing, buzzing like the bees. "Your Sanistration is at hand, Sam. Let your fear show you the way."

HARNESS BELLS

●●●● ●●●● ●●○● ○●○●

"I finished working on this thing, whatever it is," you yelled to Flora in the bathroom.

Flora yelled back something from the shower, door closed, water running.

"Yeah, that must be it." You couldn't hear a thing she said.

You trundled your mind out of that small black Bayzo box. You had been crawling around in there for days, fixing, futzing. But it was done now, how nice.

You worked on a lot of things you didn't understand. An engineer of our time. That's part of the Zen, isn't it Sam? Lost in some strange machine, foreign but familiar. You break it into parts, clean each piece, replace the broken ones, fix the connections, and put it back together. And you can make your way without really understanding anything.

The water stopped, followed by the squeaky sounds of heels on the shower floor.

Outside the black box, in your right mind again, you disconnected those Bayzos. They came away with a magnetic snap, each one linked to others, capabilities multiplied by their proximity.

Flora walked from the bathroom to the bedroom and back, towel around her head, a brief silhouette of her shapes, dripping wet as she went.

She yelled in again, over the sound of the bathroom fan.

"No, I don't think Doris Day was ever president."

Flora peeked in, head wrapped, her nakedness cut in half by the door frame. A constellation of dewy drops clung to her breast in the firelight. She tilted her chin at you, a subtle smirk, and then disappeared again.

"Well so what if it *is* a bicycle," you said. "Why would it need a protein spectrometer?"

A minute passed, and Flora came in to the main room, her smoothness covered in rough jeans, her softness wrapped in wool, a sweater, her toes in old boots. She bent over you, looking through those black boxes, seeing what you had done, how you had done it. It wasn't admiration, Sam. She was checking your work. And as she leaned in, her hair tickled your face. God Sam, she smelled like a swarm of bees, the essence of a thousand flowers dripping from the buzz in their wings.

And you were smitten Sam, as smitten as the first day, when you were just Iggy's age, a little boy who'd met a little girl.

She stood up, she moved to go, but you stood with her, tugged her close, your hand wrapped around the waist of her jeans. Her lips searched for yours, eyes closed. You tasted her breath, inches away, while your hands read the knots of her sweater, like a code in braille. Your fingers curled under her clothes, grazing the nubs of her hips and that intimate flesh just above.

"Did I pass muster?" you said.

Flora nodded yes, her mouth moving over the veins in your neck. And she found your hand, and moved it up, up, between her breasts, to her chin, and then her lips. She kissed your palm, she brought it to her cheek, rosy from the shower.

And then she drew a breath to speak, to tell you to take her, to make love to her as the last licks of daylight drained through the trees.

But you stopped her, you saw her in a knowing way, and you said "Why don't you cry for him? You cried then, before he died. But not since. Why?"

Flora was still, still like the sky, like dead air over sails.

"Maybe it would ease this. The pain," you said in gritted teeth. "Maybe you could let him go."

A long silence. What was she saying, Sam?

"I know you hurt," you said, "I've wanted so long for you to get better."

You kissed her on the cheek.

"But I've stopped believing in it."

Flora put her forehead into your shoulder. You held her, pulled her into you. Enveloped her. She had dropped anchor, unwilling to move away from the life, the waves, from the deep waters where Iggy was lost.

"What other choice do we have now?" you said.

Flora nodded. She nodded agreement. What was she agreeing to, Sam? Something long planned?

"Let's go, tonight, we'll walk," you said, "We'll sit at our spot and eat something. The sun will set on us, right out over the lake."

Flora closed her eyes. You moved to get ready, but she pulled you back. And Flora kissed you, lips on lips, a hard, tired love on her tongue. Could you hear it, Sam? A rending of wood, a shearing of metal as the ship got pulled, your full sails and her anchor. What other choice did you have, Sam? But to cut that chain.

You grabbed a bag from the fridge. And that knife, you know the one. It wasn't for cheese, Sam. And you met her at the door, you walked out together, her hand in yours. You took her away Sam, for the last, last time.

LOVELY, DARK

●●●● ●●●● ●●○● ●●○●

"Maybe she fell out of love, Sam?" I said, needling.

You were rocking on the cot, pulling those thin sheets out from under you.

"She loved me," you said, "even on that last day."

You bit at the sheets, tore them with your teeth. You needed that raw sound to keep you conscious.

"No, I mean she was out of love with the world," I said, looming over you, close enough so you could hear me breathe. Close enough so I could see your fear take over.

"Mmmmm," you said.

"What are you doing Sam, flossing?" You moved a shred of torn sheet over your teeth. "Well, that would keep anyone awake I guess," I gave you a little chuckle. I wanted to seem friendly.

"So you had to cut her away didn't you, Sam." I was soothing now. "I mean, your love was this soft music, a delicate melody, waning, waning, waning," I tapered off to silence.

And your rocking slowed, your eyes closed. I was ready to see it, mind wide open to hear those final notes. How long could you go on nervous energy? But you shot off the bed, began to dance in place. A little longer, I supposed.

You put an empty coffee cup to your lips, licking the rim for the last drop. But it had been empty for some time. The bees would only bring so much. And all that caffeine. Your mood would swing, from anxious to calm to desperate, in the span of seconds. The mind goes, Sam. And you were going. You pulled the sheets and mattress from the bed, threw them on the floor, and bounced yourself onto the thick metal springs, trying to find something to poke you in the back. You folded your elbows underneath you and pressed your weight into the bedframe, hoping to get your arm hairs stuck in the springs.

I stayed close, you knew where I was. I'm good at that, but it's easy. I could calm you down or stir you up. It doesn't matter. We knew where this was going. And I was very patient. We're both very patient men, Sam.

I picked up the shreds of ripped sheets, rubbed the coarseness between my fingers. "Sam," I said with a long calm. "Let's just ease into this thing, you don't need to hurt, my friend. Not the way you hurt Flora. You can just drift off and we'll begin."

You felt it again, the weight, the pressure of sleep, like drowning from the inside out, a skull full of warm water, pouring through your eyes.

You shook yourself, terrified, and slipped off the bed, dropped below the frame, sliding over moist tiles. It was dark down there. You pushed off on the metal posts and put your back against the wall. Pressing yourself into the corner, desperate to be alone, to sleep.

"Sam, I don't think they clean under there," I stooped over to see you. When you saw my eyes, you knew. *I can get to you there, too.* I didn't need to say it.

And so you shot up, looked around that small cell, the window, the sink, a little table to eat at. There was nowhere to hide.

But you tried, you stuffed yourself into the fireplace. How far did you get? Your head and arms scampering, pushing into that tiny nook. When you came out, I was on one knee, waiting to see your eyes. You bounced up and away again, full of energy, desperate energy, and no way to put it to good use. I know Sam, a jail cell makes for a lousy game of hide and seek.

I remember the heaving, the heavy breathing like you were running a race. But it was almost over, Sam. Your body was failing, exhaustion was going to win. It always does. And you began to cry, a deep churning cry. Because you had lost. And this terrible fear was here, in the cell. You couldn't keep it out. You cried for yourself, your blood, your pain, your needs, one last time Sam, one last cry forever.

And you stood at the fake window, looking out on a rainy day, your head getting heavy, heavy, tipping over. I stood behind you again, patiently waiting for the end.

Then something strange, that familiar buzz coming through the walls. It was the bees. The damn bees had come again. One floated through the six-sided hole in the door, the rest came in after the first had opened the way. A tray came with them, suspended by those clumsy black legs, wobbly with the weight of some indistinguishable fare. They offered you coffee but you asked for ice water instead. I guess you knew, Sam. I think you were finally giving in.

And then the bees left, sealed the cell and went out through the hole they'd come in. That lazy buzz lingered in the cracks of the walls.

"Thank you, my friends," I called after them. The bees have a poor sense of timing, Sam. And they don't get sarcasm.

You raised your head and ambled over to the table. Then you sat down at a chair, with good posture, and ate your last meal. Savored it, I would say. It looked good too, whatever it was. I thought it might have been corn, but it could have been potatoes, stomped by dirty boots. And there was a nice piece of ham, or was that the Kaiser roll. It's hard to tell. But you seemed to enjoy it. Ate every bite. Washed it down with ice water. I guess every meal would be delicious if you knew it was your last. You took it well Sam, I'll say that.

But you didn't clean up the way you like to. Just shuffled things to the side. You made a little mess, with the ice, but who could blame you. Your hands were shaking Sam, your mind was gone. It was time for you to get some rest, and for me to see how this whole thing ends.

THE ONLY OTHER SOUND

●●●● ●●●● ●●●● ●●○●

You stood up from the table, in a daze. I got up too. I rescued your mattress and sheets, replaced them on the bed.

"There you go, old friend," I took you by the shoulders and led you to that cot. You sat on the edge for a bit, looking at the fire. And I was patient. I stood away in a dark corner of that place. A man should have his last moments to himself.

You looked around the room a final time, the window, the table, the remnants of that rocking chair, and you nodded at me. And then you lay down, flat on the cot and closed your eyes.

I came to you as you beckoned. And I knelt there at the well-curb[4] as it were, all the ripples in your water gone quiet. And I was looking for that whiteness in your head, that truth that you had hidden so well. What was this secret that you didn't want to tell, even to me, your closest, truest friend?

"Mmmmm," you said. Your mind had grown very quiet.

You were anticipating something, this great end. I stared into that blackness, deeper and deeper. Did I see shapes swimming there? I came up close, my eyes closed, listening, smelling, feeling for the texture of those last memories. I heard

---

[4] Frost, *For Once, Then, Something*

a dripping in my heightened state, a plopping of water, the thaw of ice, crystals unforming and flowing away.

Drip. Was it Flora in the shower again? *Drip, drip*. The kitchen faucet as you cleaned blood from the knife? *Drip*. That frozen lake, the ice beginning to break?

I heard a final dripping and then something else, the tiny ting of metal, slipping, falling. I had opened my eyes, turned my head to see that spoon, your spoon from the table, tumbling end over end, and clattering to the floor, metal curves banging on the stone. And I had spun myself, been distracted all at once. A carefully planned diversion. How clever, Sam.

You were already in the air, a cat's sense of flight. Meticulous in a predatory way. The strike had happened before I could brace myself. I hit the table teeth first. And I swallowed something, a chunk of tongue maybe. It slithered as it went. The table took my eye, and the first wisps of pain arrived. But I smiled Sam, a sweetheart's smile. I could see Flora in the waves of your rage.

She was walking with you, hands clasped, the night full. Fifteen hours yet to pass on this, the darkest evening, the most darkness of the year. Then an image of Flora, but she was distant, a dim ghost, the empty woods around her. You'd parted, I surmised from the still frame of your memory. And then I knew, Sam. I saw you with that knife in your hand and I knew it all at once.

A bag of blood, sloshing with Flora's life. Filled clumsily with Iggy's old needles and a thin rubber tube meant for a little boy. Half a liter, Sam. That's how much blood Flora lost. All that the plasma bag could carry. Then that knife again, shaking, your arms buzzing to tear the plastic open, to spill that blood with rage for Iggy's damn disease. It stole your son, it withered your love. And so you shredded that bag, opened it up, and Flora bled without bleeding, into a pool in the snow. Then something I had seen before, your bloody hands and a trail of red drops. But you must have been walking backward, Sam. You were making the trail, not following it. You let that blood fall, dripping a path to your own door. And you burned the evidence in the fireplace, leaving clues that would lead us to your guilt.

You framed yourself, Sam. You must have come to believe that Flora wasn't so broken. She was sane enough to know that the hardest part of loss is change, moving on from that spiritual place, leaving your love behind. The ugly idea that time *does* heal us, and memories *do* fade. That's the real profanity of loss, Sam. That she missed Iggy badly. But she missed him a little less each day. And so she dropped her anchor, became still, held fast in that disappearing state.

And you loved her Sam, enough to burn the sails of your happy life. To stay with her in some desolate grief. Flora would never be better, so you made yourself worse. You orchestrated this, your Sanistration, a killing from the inside out. A suicide you can look in the eyes. All to hold your boat together, circling forever on the very spot where Iggy disappeared beneath the waves.

The murder was an illusion too, Sam. Flora wasn't dead, but far away. Biding her time.

I came to, in the prison cell, and finally I knew. But you were wrapping the hem of that sheet, the ripped seam, weaving it around my neck. Where had you hid that away, Sam? I had watched you so closely. You and I, we're careful men. And I thought you were crumbling Sam, but you were preparing for this end. Just as I'd hoped.

You wrapped that strong cloth seam around and around my neck and you held me down, beat me, shuffled me toward that deep, weightless end.

"Yesss..." a gurgle escaped, "...SSSam," escaping.

My nose and mouth burst a redness, they cast a sloppy shadow on the stone.

"I knew... I knew you," I was gasping here, now.

A fist, an elbow, your weight behind them, they hit my remaining eye, cut it open, slit it wide, a gaping gash.

"could... could," a labor for breath.

I spit black tar and teeth, blood and bile and saliva spread on the floor, wet my back and clothes, my gray jumpsuit, just like yours, Sam.

"do... this."

And now I'm crying, I reach for your hand, I weep and touch your face, the last embrace of brothers departing. You search my eyes, your eyes. You see that death, our death, as you would in a mirror, hands around your own neck. My mind fails, fuzzy, the white light wanes. A black snow comes, falls, accumulates in empty space. My lovely darkness at last.

MILES TO GO

●●●● ●●●● ●●●● ●●●●

You'll be asleep when Judy comes to get you, maybe passed out under the table, in that pool of my blood. Or on top of me, sprawled on my chest, your hands still tugging at the hem of that bedsheet around my neck. She'll come in and wake you, pull you up to your feet.

"I'm tired," you'll say, a whisper, hoarse from the act.

"I know," Judy will be calming, "you can sleep on the way."

The bees will be there. They'll have let Judy in, and they'll clean things up after you've left. They'll help to put you on Judy's shoulder, their clumsy little legs tugging at your flesh. And from your feet you can take a last look. Capture another snapshot in your mind. An image of your lifeless self, of your own face with those wide marble eyes. It's madness isn't it, to kill yourself and survive the ordeal. A cleansing of the spirit. A Sanistration of the will.

Judy and the bees will walk you up those stairs, climb you out of that dankness where you lived and died for days. When you reach the top, what will you see, Sam? That long hallway leading to the exit. And Lou, the bailiff, an old man. He'll be holding a white box, you remember the one. He'll put his hand on your shoulder and open it for you. What will you see inside, Sam? Something you haven't seen in days. It's a mirror! A silvery thing, clean and bright. A stark reflection of the man that's staring in.

"Cry for that man, if the tears will come." Those are the words, Sam. Lou will whisper them in your ear, as he always does. And they'll sound as if they come from somewhere inside, as if they boil up from your belly.

But what can you feel for him, that man in the reflection, the one you killed. Can you weep for him now, after what he did?

Crying is a selfish act, Sam. But I've cured you of that. Made you selfless in grief. You're like Flora now. I suppose that's what you wanted, Sam. I suppose that's how you planned it.

That's why I needed to become you. To know what you knew. So that when you killed me, I would die with your truth. Innocence is a lie. The only way out of Sanistration is through guilt. You once told me you weren't a killer, Sam. That you were an innocent man. Now what do you believe?

You won't shed a tear, Sam. You'll close the box and leave the Secure Sanistration Wing of the Mantis Center for Criminal Correction. You'll be a free man. Judy will walk you out to a transport there. She'll treat you kindly, a hand on your arm. And her thumb will be just fine, Sam. Not a stitch or a scar. You'll climb aboard and settle in. You're safe now, Sam. Dead and empty and well again.

When you arrive on that mountain, you'll see a slender plume of smoke. It'll be trickling up from the chimney of your little cabin. You'll walk up that cobbled path, spring all around you, a thaw on the frozen lake and sunlight dripping through the woods.

You'll go inside, home at last, and you'll find a warm fire, an invitation from someone who's missed you. Though as you promised, it hasn't been long. And Flora will bring you to the window, made of real wood and real glass, that looks over the lake. She'll point to the pier there, and you'll see the Black Alder, your sail boat. The hull held up against the ice. She'll have pulled it back Sam, tied it safely to those wet wooden posts.

That little boat waited through the winter. And it may sit again for some time, rocking in light waves. Weathering the rain. But you and Flora will be together now, each of you back from some dark wood, some lonely place. Allied in a long war, against your own terrible grief. And no one knows for sure. But I have this hope, Sam. That one day those still skies will give way to a gentle wind, the anchor will come up, and the Black Alder will sail again.

Honorable Mentions

Submissions for this anthology far outstripped the number of stories we could effectively publish. And so, out of necessity, the editorial staff was extremely selective. The authors found herein produced the best work. But in the section below, we list of few of the stand-out stories that we thought deserved some measure of merit. Look for these authors elsewhere, especially as their work matures.

Harlan Ellison	I HAVE NO MOUTH, AND I MUST SCREAM
Arthur C. Clarke	THE NINE BILLION NAMES OF GOD
Ursula K Le Guin	THE WORD FOR WORLD IS FOREST
Ray Bradbury	THERE WILL COME SOFT RAINS
Robert A. Heinlein	THE GREEN HILLS OF EARTH
Kurt Vonnegut	HARRISON BERGERON
Isaac Asimov	THE LAST QUESTION
William Gibson	BURNING CHROME
Philip K. Dick	MINORITY REPORT
Larry Niven	NEUTRON STAR

And a final thanks you to our
family, friends, and readers.
We write for you.

www.ingramcontent.com/pod-product-compliance
Lightning Source LLC
Chambersburg PA
CBHW020559310726
48979CB00008B/1273/J